Just William
Through the Ages

Mary Cadogan

Just William
Through the Ages

MACMILLAN

To Darrell Swift
and the Northern Old Boys' Book Club
with thanks for many happy
William days

ACKNOWLEDGEMENTS

The author and publishers wish to thank David Schutte for his generous help in supplying illustration material and Mrs Joan Baverstock for permission to use both the photograph of Thomas Henry in the Foreword and his painting of William which is reproduced on the jacket.

The publishers also wish to thank the family of Richmal Crompton for permission to use her photograph in the Foreword.

The frontispiece and the cartoons on pages 28–9 and 60–61 are from the *Happy Mag* Christmas 1925, Christmas 1926 and April 1940 respectively.

Copyright © 1994 Mary Cadogan

Thomas Henry illustrations copyright © Thomas Henry Fisher Estate
Henry Ford illustrations copyright © Macmillan Children's Books

Quotations from the writings of Richmal Crompton by permission of
A.P. Watt Ltd and the Richmal Crompton Estate

First published 1994 by
Macmillan Publishers Limited
Cavaye Place London SW10 9PG
and Basingstoke

Associated companies throughout the world

ISBN 0-333-62097-6

The right of Mary Cadogan to be identified as the author of this work has been asserted by her in accordance with the Copyright, Designs and Patents Act 1988.

Photoset by Parker Typesetting Service, Leicester
Printed in Hong Kong

Contents

Foreword

Mention 'Just William' and people immediately picture a boy, a rather scruffy one, with a look which is both devil-may-care and firmly confident. He is wearing a cap with blue and white circular bands, the peak over one ear. His tie, knitted and square-ended, is roughly knotted some inches below a curiously rumpled and crooked collar. He wears grey flannel shorts and knee-high socks with turn-over tops, which collapse in wrinkles at the ankles. He is always untidy, and frequently muddy. But this figure is not just a memory from childhood stories, in the way that little girls with long straight fair hair may suggest Alice. This is a lively character who can fit into all manner of present-day situations the like of which his creator, Richmal Crompton, could never have envisaged. Journalists adapt his words, and his approach to life, to fit modern happenings, and cartoonists use his well-known outlines to illustrate the doings of prominent figures in the news.

My aunt, Richmal Crompton Lamburn, born in Bury, Lancashire, in 1890, created the character of William. Thomas Henry Fisher, born in Nottingham in 1879, was the artist selected by the publishers, Newnes, to illustrate her stories and he created the visual image of William that is known not only throughout the English-speaking world but also in many other countries. The two of them presented William and his escapades to readers for forty-three years. It was not until 1958 that a meeting was arranged between them, and there is no record that they even corresponded before that. It had, perhaps, never seemed necessary.

A friendly relationship developed between Richmal Crompton and the Fishers from that meeting and they corresponded until the artist's death in 1962. The friendship, however, in no way changed their independent way of working. They were more likely to write about their gardens, the weather and family health than about William, though Richmal Crompton would never fail to praise Thomas Henry's work as new books were published. He realized for the first time that Newnes did not ask for her comments on his dust-jackets, and that any criticisms he had received did not come from her!

There is very little description of William in the books. He is never introduced to the reader: he just appears, as if we had always known him. At first, Thomas Henry portrayed him as a comparatively orderly character. His socks were rarely even crumpled, no matter what he had been up to, and his cap often sat squarely on his

head. By the late 1930s, his socks had taken on the familiar concertina line that made my grandmother despair of Mrs Brown's ability to turn a heel properly. The cap had become a token piece of fabric resting apparently by faith on William's tousled mop.

The chief thing about William that Richmal Crompton does find words for is his hair, which is normally 'like a neglected lawn' and even after severe brushings soon returns to 'its favourite vertical angle'. Thomas Henry did not fail to do justice to this. Indeed, by the mid 1930s both William's hair and his skull protrude distinctively, well beyond a normal boy's. She describes his expressions, and the quite horrible faces he can pull. Otherwise, she probably just saw him as a boy, dressed much like any other boy, at least as he left his home. She created the character; Thomas Henry created his appearance. (Goodness knows who created the impression, to be seen everywhere in competitions for look-alikes during the Centenary Year, that William was always sticking out his tongue. He was rarely so crude, especially when grown-ups were watching.) Thomas Henry had a masterly gift for conveying an expression, hopeful, ingratiating, threatening, spellbound, excited, nonchalant, belligerent, boastful – these and a thousand more are there in the drawings.

While both author and illustrator had a marvellous grasp of character, and could convey it with a few strokes of the pen, it cannot be said that they were equally sure over facts. Richmal Crompton tried to write about activities which were within her own experience, but times kept changing. She steadfastly refused to become involved with science fiction, though her publishers wanted her to keep up to date with children's enthusiasms. She would go no further than a space animal fancy-dress costume and a moon rocket attraction in a fairground. After a large number of letters pointing out inconsistencies in the stories, she would make some attempt to list her characters and where and how they appeared, but she could not sustain it for very long. She was not really interested in what Mr Brown did at his office or, indeed, what any of the people did when away from William. She would have been amazed, and very impressed, at Kenneth Waller's researches. He has not only made a convincing case for the whereabouts of William's village, but even mapped it with all its features, and planned William's house. My aunt would not have believed it possible! One begins to forget it is only a story.

William's house was not like anywhere Richmal Crompton had ever lived, except just possibly one of the vicarages where her father used to give his family a summer holiday while he looked after the

COMPANY COMING!

THE MAN IN POSSESSION.

parish and took the services. Their own home was a much more modest place, with no garden to speak of. The greenhouse, stable, library, morning-room and all the rest were conjured up to meet the passing needs of the Brown family, not because they were part of the world to which my aunt was herself accustomed. The host of servants in the house, too, came from outside her own experience.

I was disconcerted when a young man once told me how much he enjoyed learning about the social background of earlier years from the books. I was afraid he might have been misled. Some institutions and customs my aunt wrote about are ones she remembered from her childhood and did not realize were now unfamiliar. Others are things she inquired about but in some way misunderstood. Of course, many are still exactly right. In the last story in *William – the Lawless*, written in 1968, she never doubted that a family returning from a seaside holiday would still send the luggage to the station by the carrier and themselves travel there by bus, and assumed that on a sponsored walk it is those who walk the fastest who raise the most money for the cause. She never attempted to keep pace with all the changes in the English educational system when describing William's schooling, and was shocked when I once suggested that his school now resembled a small comprehensive, of one of the more unorthodox varieties. On the other hand, city-dwellers may be surprised to learn that there is nothing out of date in a small rural grammar school having a house of boarders. Some in East Anglia only closed theirs in the 1980s.

Similarly, Thomas Henry's drawings do not always match the text of the stories. Boots become shoes, jackets become pullovers, gates and fences are misplaced. Most surprising of all are the variations in the appearance of Jumble, himself almost as unforgettable as William. Originally he appears 'fox-terrier ears cocked, retriever nose raised, collic tail wagging, slightly dachshund body a-quiver with the joy of life'. The ears grow longer and fuller through the series until they come close to those of Thomas Henry's own beloved springer spaniels. Richmal Crompton herself bowed to the irresistible and changed the tail to 'nondescript'. Sometimes he appears white with black patches, at others almost entirely black, and even, by the cover of *William – the Explorer*, largely brown.

Curiously, these things do not seem to matter very much. William's adventures, as recorded by Richmal Crompton and Thomas Henry, cover fifty years, and in all that time he never grows any older. The world about him changed considerably between 1919 and 1969. Fashions in what people did, and how they did them, came and went. William took it all in his stride. He might have found this more difficult had he been identified precisely with any particular period or set of ways, instead of being left to confront all that came in his own inimitable way.

RICHMAL ASHBEE

Opposite: *Give-away plates from Christmas 1925* Sunny Mag.

Introduction

Richmal Crompton's untidy, opinionated but aspirational and optimistic anti-hero, William Brown, was created seventy-five years ago when 'Rice-Mould' – the first story to feature him – was published in the *Home Magazine* of February 1919. Since then the eleven-year-old character whom she once categorized as a 'pot-boiler' has become a household word and an archetype of the inquiring, adventurous, outdoor child.

William's personality is so vivid that it is indeed sometimes difficult to remember that he is the product of Richmal's story-spinning skills and not a real boy. However, although we cannot actually see him in the flesh, stamped on our minds is the indelibly authentic image of him in every possible mood and situation, as drawn by Thomas Henry with a flair that matches the author's exuberant narratives. In fact, Thomas Henry was not the saga's original artist. 'Rice-Mould' was illustrated by Louise Hocknell, who invested William with a winsome charm that was not exactly appropriate for his anarchic nature. Various illustrators and cartoonists were then asked to submit drawings based on Richmal's character descriptions, and Thomas Henry was chosen to provide the pictures for William's future exploits. He was to draw him with undiminished relish and vigour for over forty years, until his death in the early 1960s. The writer and illustrator relationship between Richmal and himself was as perfect a partnership as that of Arthur Conan Doyle and Sydney Paget (for Sherlock Holmes) or Frank Richards and C. H. Chapman (for Billy Bunter).

William's author and artist were both to become well known by their first two names only. Richmal Crompton Lamburn was born at Bury in Lancashire in November 1890 and died in 1969; she was writing about William until the day before her death. Thomas Henry Fisher was born at Eastwood in Nottingham in June 1879 and died in 1962, soon after posting to the publishers his latest drawing for *William and the Witch*. He was already an established artist and cartoonist before he began to draw William, and as well as visually interpreting Richmal's long-running stories he continued to contribute cartoons and pictures to a wide variety of publications including *Punch*, *Tatler*, the *Strand Magazine*, *Little Folks* and the *Boy's Own Paper*. After his sudden death from a heart-attack a replacement artist had to be found quickly to provide the rest of the illustrations for *William and the Witch*. Henry Ford took over from then until the stories ended, and – with some measure of success – valiantly endeavoured to emulate Thomas Henry's style.

Richmal Crompton produced thirty-eight William books, most of which were collections of her magazine stories, written originally for adults but subsequently taken over by children. She wrote a similar number of adult novels of the family-saga type. These, though perceptively produced and engagingly atmospheric of their period, never achieved the celebrity and addictiveness of the William tales. With hindsight her anti-hero's escapades can be seen as virtual parodies of her adult novels: as drawing-room dramas transmogrified into robust comedy, with William ingenuously precipitating social chaos and embarrassment for his elders.

The world which he inhabited was in many ways very different from that of the 1990s, but the quintessentially imaginative world of childhood – so graphically expressed in and by William – has not changed. He is not the product of a place or period that is absolutely specific (it is significant that Richmal never named or clearly located William's

that it was he who 'took and held the field' with a tenacious and sturdy life of his own.

Like all great literary characters, William is multi-faceted, and *Just William Through the Ages* is an attempt to focus on different aspects of his personality, relationships and aspirations over the decades. Of course the stories were written primarily to entertain (some critics have assessed them as the funniest books of the twentieth century), but they are also rich in sharply observed social comment. William's village is a microcosm of the world at large; we could apply to it the one-time slogan of a national newspaper which specializes in startling revelations – 'All human life is there.' It is intriguing to look at the social changes which are reflected in the saga. In between the two world wars, for example, leisured ladies of William's acquaintance not only arranged garden fêtes, sales of work, pageants and children's parties but also promoted élitist literary societies and esoterically uplifting groups. The 1940s brought a wartime sense of solidarity as well as the challenges of some drastic social upheavals, while in the post-war period the denizens of William's village find themselves involved with protest marchers, the problems of the National Health Service, planning regulations and bureaucracy.

Some things, however, never change. William and the Outlaws are frequently bitten with reforming zeal, and having to fight battles for fresh causes – but they remain perpetual symbols of straightforward and appealing youth, as Richmal Crompton so perceptively conveyed:

village), but he speaks for boys and girls everywhere. Like all children, as well as being resilient he is vulnerable, and his appeal springs partly from the fact that he represents juvenile openness and candour up against the double standards of authoritative adults. Satisfyingly, however, he is the underdog who generally manages to come out on top of the heap. He is a country child, but as he skirmishes with the stereotypical characters in his village or explores the ditches, fields and woods around his fairly spacious home, children who live in suburbs, towns and cities have no difficulty in identifying with him.

Richmal originally thought that William was her puppet and that she pulled the strings. She soon realized, however,

> 'What'll we do this morning?' said
> Ginger. It was sunny. It was holiday
> time. They had each other and a dog.
> Boyhood could not wish for more. The
> whole world lay before them.

Above: The first pictorial representation of William, drawn by Louise Hocknell for the story 'Rice-Mould'.

JUST — WILLIAM

THE MOST POPULAR *William* BOY IN FICTION

THOMAS HENRY

BY RICHMAL CROMPTON

The 1920s – William the Innocent

'Rice-Mould' was the first William story to be published (in the *Home Magazine* of February 1919). However, 'William Goes to the Pictures', which appeared in the same periodical two months later, was reputedly the very first William exploit that Richmal Crompton wrote and, appropriately, when the tales were collected into books, it became the opening episode of *Just – William*, which was published in May 1922. 'Rice-Mould' found its way into the second book, *More William*, which came out at the end of the same year. The stories continued to appear regularly in the *Home Magazine* until October 1922 when they moved to the *Happy Mag*, which was to remain their regular home until the magazine folded in May 1940, a victim of the paper shortages of the Second World War.

The stories from 1919 to the end of the 1920s are collected in nine other books besides *Just – William* and *More William*: these are *William Again*, *William – the Fourth*, *Still – William*, *William – the Conqueror*, *William – the Outlaw*, *William – in Trouble*, *William – the Good*, *William* and *William – the Bad*. The *Home Magazine* and *Happy Mag* were the kind of monthlies that appealed to the whole family. Richmal's satiric style and allusive vocabulary were appreciated by – and indeed aimed at – adult readers, but children as well as their parents were turning with relish to the pages that carried the regular William story. The editorial staff of these Newnes magazines got the message, and when the stories began to appear between hard covers they were packaged primarily to appeal to the juvenile market.

These comically sparkling tales of the 1920s set the scene for the whole saga. As Richmal Ashbee says in her foreword (see page 6), William is not at first described: he is just there, as if we have always known him, but as the decade progresses he, his family, friends, enemies and associates, become fully fleshed out – and so too do their physical environs.

The saga's main and most resilient characters are launched. We get to know William's immediate family – his slightly irascible father and serene, perpetually sock-mending, mother, his sister Ethel, the gorgeous good-time girl, and his ever-susceptible student brother, Robert. His sturdy henchmen – Ginger, Henry and Douglas – unfold as separate personalities despite their

THE HAPPY MAG.

SEPTEMBER

7D

"PERCY, I KNOW WHO IT DO TAKE YOUR CLAMM HAND OFF MY NECK!"

bonding with William and the docilely adoring Joan into the group known as the Outlaws. We meet the notorious *nouveaux riches*, rotund and rubicund Mr and Mrs Bott and their pretty but precocious offspring, Violet Elizabeth; also Hubert Lane, William's spoilt and slimily smug arch-enemy; then there are those stalwart pillars of the local community – the frosty, fussy and child-hating Miss Milton, the earnest Vicar and his somewhat officious helpmate, Mr and Mrs Monks, and General Moult, the bristly Boer War veteran of peppery disposition and firmly static opinions. And as well as the leading lights, the 1920s stories provide a large and colourful supporting cast of erudite aesthetes, nervous novelists and junior clerics, intense and/or vinegary spinsters, batty artists and bright young things. There is an equally zestful conveyance of their physical setting as William's unnamed, archetypal, quintessentially English and elastic village takes shape, with its manor house, workmen's cottages, cinema, sweetshop, dogs, ditches and surrounding woods, fields, crumbling barns, sheep, cows – and, of course, irate farmers.

It seems particularly appropriate that William came into being in 1919, the year which immediately followed the ending of the Great War. It was, after the long period of tragedy and despair, a time of expansiveness and optimism, and the general mood is reflected in William's personality. In these early stories he also has an innocence which began to desert him once he had acquired more experience of the devious ways of pompous or conniving adults. Thomas Henry's illustrations show him as smaller, tidier and more vulnerable at the beginning of the decade than he is at its end. From the start of the saga he causes domestic chaos – but this is disruptiveness brought about by good intentions and guileless belief in the honesty of hypocritical adults: there is no malice or deliberate destruction in William, even when his antics are at their most anarchic.

His helpfulness-going-astray is evident from the first episode of *Just – William*. In 'William Goes to the Pictures' he is unusually affluent. He has just received a shilling from an aunt (for posting a letter and carrying home her groceries) and decides to spend half of this on his favourite sweets, Gooseberry Eyes, and the other half on a visit to the cinema. (At this time film-going was still, for many people, a novelty and a treat: we are told that William had only been to 'the Picture Palace once before in his life'.) His desire to share the two immensely pleasurable experiences of sucking Gooseberry Eyes and savouring those cinematic thrills and chills results in his making Joan, the little girl next door, ill, in the exacerbation of his father's liverish headache, in his telling a young man whose affections are

WILLIAM WAS HAPPILY AND QUIETLY ENGAGED IN BURNING THE PAINT OFF HIS BEDROOM DOOR.

elsewhere engaged that Ethel is besotted with him, and in him doing serious damage to his bedroom door by burning and hacking the paint off it. But he is motivated throughout by his characteristically firm conviction that he is being helpful. William reviews the day's events as a series of misunderstandings on the part of the grown-ups who are involved, and particularly by the 'violent and unreasonable parent' (his father) who has in the end 'brutally assaulted' him. Mr Brown, of course, considers that he has acted with as much forbearance as anyone could be expected to show under the onslaught of William's activities. He confides to his wife, with one hand 'pressed to his aching brow, and the other gesticulating freely, "He's insane . . . stark, raving insane"' and, after detailing once again his younger son's offences, declares 'They're the acts of a lunatic – you ought to have his brain examined.' Mrs Brown, however, is not only more placid but more realistic. She is, in this first chapter of the first book, already engaged in her apparently favourite occupation of sock-mending or -making, and temporarily laying aside her work she says mildly, 'It certainly sounds very silly, dear . . . But there might be some explanation of it all, if only we knew. Boys are such funny things.'

The characters of William and his parents are thus immediately conveyed in the simple shorthand of this episode. William's optimism runs parallel with his innocence and is satisfyingly unquenchable. In *More William* (1922), for example, he is erecting a rabbit-hutch in the back garden: 'He hoped that if he made a hutch, Providence would supply a rabbit.' More prosaically, in *William Again* (1923), he hopes to break his parentally imposed pattern of church-going: '"I'm not going to church this morning," Robert happened to say, carrying a deck-chair into the garden. "An' I'm not, either," said William, as he seized another chair . . .' On this occasion, however, although always eventually resilient, his optimism takes one of those nasty knocks which his father frequently administers. William

"GOOD MORNIN', FATHER," SAID WILLIAM WITH WHAT HE FONDLY IMAGINED TO BE A COURTLY MANNER.

explains that he'd *like* to go to church and is indeed disappointed that he feels too ill to do so:

> . . . his Pegasean imagination soared aloft on daring wings – 'I feel 's if I might *die* if I went to church this morning feelin' 's ill as I do now.'
>
> 'If you're as bad as that,' Mr Brown said callously as he brushed his coat, 'I suppose you might as well die in church as anywhere.'

In the face of such unsympathetic grown-up behaviour it is to William's credit that he retains his basic trust in positive aspects of life, and his belief in the power of his own will and imagination. These are put severely to the test in *William – the Good* (1928) when the

"GOLLY!" SAID GINGER WISTFULLY, "JUST THINK OF
PLAYIN' WITH EM."

"WHAT WOULD YOU LIKE MOST IN THE WORLD?" HE
SAID SUDDENLY. "WHITE RATS!" SAID WILLIAM
WITHOUT A MOMENT'S HESITATION.

Outlaws, in their usual impecunious state with their pocket-money mortgaged to pay for breakages, are lusting after an eight-and-sixpenny set of brass-topped cricket stumps in the window of the village's general shop. Although they have in the past made do with wickets chalked on trees or sticks stuck in the ground, once they have seen this set of stumps 'de luxe . . . from the Land of the Ideal' they feel that their game will lose all its savour if they can't possess them. However, to Ginger, Henry and Douglas it seems as impossible to raise eight shillings and sixpence as to raise a fortune. William, irritated by their 'spiritless attitude', swaggeringly promises to find the money before the end of the day. He does, too! At first his efforts to beg, borrow or earn money from his family go horribly wrong, and, running out of inspiration, he goes with his mother to a sale of work arranged by Miss Milton. Ethel is there, accompanied by a determined (but nameless) 'young man with projecting teeth' who connives with the 'fortune-teller' (his own sister) to hint heavily to Ethel that it will be to her enormous and lasting advantage to respond positively to the request of someone who is soon to present her with a gift. Of course he plans to propose. William, peeping under the fortune-telling booth and hearing everything, beats the toothy admirer to it, gives Ethel the present of a bag of monkey-nuts – and then asks meekly if she will let him have eight and six. Remembering the intensity of the fortune-teller's pronouncement she dare not refuse – though she is amazed and infuriated by William's cheek. At the end of the afternoon he airily hands the stupefied and amazed Outlaws the beautiful brass-topped cricket stumps: 'It was a moment worth living for. William felt that he really didn't care *what* happened after that.'

Despite the frustrations that his brother and sister so often heap upon him, William's optimism even embraces his relationship with them. Ethel is very much a 1920s bright young thing, a fetching but work-shy 'flapper' whose main interests are parties, dancing, fashions and flirting. Her red-gold hair and lustrous blue eyes captivate by turns every unmarried man in the village and every eligible bachelor who visits it. Her age remains static (at nineteen); she thrives on adoration from the opposite sex, enjoys playing off one admirer against another, loves queening it over her courtiers and is frequently bitchy about her girl-friends and spiteful towards William (whose cock-eyed helpfulness, of course, can be mind-blowingly aggravating to someone like Ethel who has a high-flown image of herself to maintain). William has an almost morbid interest in her conquests. He is prepared – by fair but more likely by foul means – to further the cause of any ardent swain who is ready to hand him generous tips in the erroneous assumption that Ethel will be influenced by her younger brother's opinion. One of the first young men whom she enslaves by fluttering her eyelashes and tossing her flaming hair is Mr James French in *Just – William*. He is good-looking, with the sartorial elegance of the period that appeals to the always impeccably groomed and stylish Ethel. Well suited and shod, he wears spats and carries a walking cane. His plan to get into his beloved's good graces is straightforward. William is to accompany her to the shops and offer to carry her purchases home; on the way back he is to collapse – ostensibly because of feeling ill – when James will appear, offer to carry home Ethel's heavy parcels and thus earn her gratitude. All goes according to plan, except that he has to carry William as well as the packages home, but his accomplice's chosen reward of two white rats causes havoc in the Brown household: that night, when Ethel awakens to find a rat pawing her celebrated tresses, and in church the following morning, when the other rodent jumps out of William's pocket during the hymn, runs up Mr Brown's body and settles on his balding head, into which it digs its claws. Not surprisingly, James French is only briefly in favour with Ethel.

Several books and some years later in *Still – William* (1925), William is trying

"NOW, DON'T BE FRIGHTENED, LITTLE GIRL," SAID MR. MARCH. "I KNOW HOW YOUR LITTLE HEART BEATS AT THE THOUGHT OF YOUR GEORGE."
"MR. MARCH!" EXCLAIMED ETHEL, "ARE YOU ILL?"

very positively to get Ethel married. By this time he has become far more aware of his sister's limitations and likes the idea of her going off to live somewhere else. His choice of potential husband is a stumpy, sparse-haired, short-sighted, arch and pompous young man named Mr March, who is not only 'gone on Ethel' but has 'gotter lot of money an' a nice garden an' a big house'. William is quite convinced that he is doing his sister a favour in cooking up a compli-cated and, in Ethel's eyes, a dreadfully embarrassing match-making plan.

Her furious threat to 'tell father' and her impassioned plea to her mother ('. . . can't we do anything about William? Can't we send him to an orphanage . . .?') are constantly repeated as the saga progresses. So too are the sentiments in William's disillusioned response:

'I've took a lot of trouble trying to get her married . . . and this is how she pays me!' . . . He looked at the indignant figure of his pretty nineteen-year-old-sister which was still visible in the distance and added gloomily: 'She's turning out an old maid an' it's not my fault. I've done my best. Seems to me she's goin' to go on livin' in our house all her life till she dies, an' that's a nice look out for me, isn't it?'

Nevertheless he continues to be active on her behalf although his interference in her romantic and social life is nearly always disastrous – particularly on those occasions when he most wants to help. In *William – the Good* (1928), for example, his natural rude health has been temporarily weakened by a bout of influenza so that he not only reads but is deeply influenced by a book in the ministering-children tradition which a great-aunt has sent him. Its hero is a boy of William's age whose angelic character makes him the sunshine of his home. He converts his elder sister – who drinks and steals – from her life of sin and crime to one of virtue.

William sees Ethel taking a generous

"OH, ETHEL'S NOT ILL OR ANYTHING!" SAID WILLIAM.
"IT'S ONLY THAT SHE DRINKS."
"W-WHAT?" SAID MRS. MORTON.

swig from a bottle of cough mixture (unknown to him she thinks she has a cold coming on and is anxious to ward it off until she has auditioned for the role of Juliet with the local amateur dramatic society). William decides that she is a secret alcoholic. An overheard conversation between her and Mrs Brown, which he misunderstands, convinces him that she is also a kleptomaniac. His earnest desire to help her prompts him to convey this information to some of the dramatic society personnel who attend the auditions for *Romeo and Juliet*. It is no wonder that Ethel is often driven to declare that he is mad, while even the usually unruffled Mrs Brown is forced, on another occasion (in *Still – William*) when he has upset, embarrassed and infuriated his sister, to ask 'But William . . . how did you think it was going to help anyone to say Ethel had epilepsy and consumption?'

Although a state of guerrilla warfare often appears to exist between William and his older brother, he actually has real affection for, and strong moments of rapport with, Robert who, like Ethel, is a fairly lightweight character but at least – when urged on by his more intellectual friends – will take some interest in poetry, politics, serious issues and higher things. His age shifts during the course of the saga between seventeen and twenty-one and, apart from a brief period of military service (see page 59), he remains a perpetual student. His hobbies are his motorbike, football, tennis, badminton – and most of all those numerous embodiments of 'the most beautiful girl he has ever met'. William often tries to help Robert's affairs along but his intervention in his brother's love-life is usually disruptive, if not actually disastrous. He confuses Robert's discarded amours with the current one, composes atrocious (though well-intentioned) romantic verses to the wrong girl on more than one occasion and, by his mere grubby and loquacious presence when Robert is wooing some new 'goddess', humiliates him frightfully.

William has scant respect for the appealing creatures who captivate his

WILLIAM— THE GOOD

RICHMAL CROMPTON

THE MOST POPULAR *William* BOY IN FICTION

WILLIAM'S SMALL HEAD WAS CRANED ROUND ROBERT'S ARM. "I LIKE THINGS WHAT GROW QUICK, DON'T YOU?" HE SAID – ALL INNOCENT ANIMATION.

ST. WILLIAM STOOD UP TO PREACH TO THE RELUCTANT JUMBLE. "DEARLY BELOVED JUMBLE," HE BEGAN.

brother, and astutely recognizes the domineering streaks that lie beneath their apparent fragile femininity, their vanity and self-absorption. However, there are times when he identifies with Robert's infatuations and is a rival for the inamorata's affections. The first instance of this comes in *Just – William* when Miss Cannon (the first girl on record to stir Robert to passion) comes to tea. William falls victim to her charms when she dallies with him to play Red Indians on her way into the house. During the agonizingly genteel and inhibited tea-party which follows, he resolutely sits in on Robert's fumbled and frustrated attempts to converse in a sparkling way with her. Things come to a head when his family endeavours surreptitiously to remove William from Robert's love-blighted chat with Miss Cannon, and he protests in a stentorian stage-whisper: 'I wasn't doin' any harm . . . only *speaking* to her! . . . Is no one else ever to *speak* to her . . . jus' cause Robert's fell in love with her?' Alas, poor Robert!

William's basic nonconformity and capacity to create an 'underground' society are frequently shown in the books of the 1920s, when they are in sharp contrast with the polite and decorous middle-class values that held sway around him. The Outlaws, as their name suggests, are themselves an 'alternative' organization and they often experiment with new social structures and modes of behaviour. In *William – the Conqueror* (1926) they are – briefly – inspired by the activities of St Francis of Assisi in an episode called 'William Leads a Better Life'. They are attracted to the outdoor, wandering anti-authoritarian life after long-continuing problems with the French language – and of course their French master. William decides that he would 'a lot sooner be a saint and build things an' cook things an' preach to things than keep goin' to school an' learnin' the same ole things day after day . . . things like French verbs without any sense in them'. So, garbed somewhat uncomfortably in their made-to-accommodate-growth dressing-gowns, the Outlaws became friars or

'Williamcans' in the steps of the Franciscans.

Of course they soon come up against the problems which beset prophets, preachers and proselytizers: their audience is not ready for their message. Humans sneer and jeer – and even 'brother Jumble' and the 'sister hens' of the animal kingdom whom they address are hardly appreciative. And then there is the difficulty of the Williamcans satisfying their basic material needs. They start off, as they think St Francis did, by selling (actually pawning) some things belonging to their fathers which buys them a first meal of sweets, cream buns, liquorice water, etc., but on the whole their experiences as holy men are neither enjoyable nor uplifting. It gets cold and starts to rain; they are chilly and hungry, and battered and bruised after having to fight some village children who've goaded them about their curious appearance. When Ginger piously points out that if they are true Williamcans they should really give their last sixpence to the poor, their leader has had enough: '"Well . . . I'm just about sick of bein' a saint, I'd sooner be a pirate or a Red Indian any day." The rest looked relieved . . .'

In *William – in Trouble* (1927), our hero's slightly cock-eyed and protective idealism inspires some very down-to-earth dealings with the fairies that spring from the best of motives but go sadly awry. He inadvertently gate-crashes into a girls' boarding-school, and is at first taken for the gardener's boy who has been coerced into modelling for the art-class: the teacher tells her students, 'I want you to draw him as he is – just an ugly, dirty little boy', and William's apoplectic fury at this insult is prevented from finding immediate and violent expression because a dark-haired and dimpled girl (of the type to which he is always susceptible) defends him. When the class ends he explains to her that he is not the gardener's boy but an intrepid adventurer: 'I've explored places where no white man ever set his feet before.' She seems morose – and unimpressed by his boast – so he goes on to say that he's run

'terrible risks from starvation an' wild animals' and, as she still seems unresponsive, declares – untruthfully – for good measure that he once had all his teeth out without gas. Eventually he discovers that her depression is caused by homesickness, and she wants to get out of performing that day in the school play so that she can go home for a short visit. He nobly offers to take on her part. It is, however, the role of 'Fairy Daffodil' and the little girl rightly protests that he doesn't remotely resemble a fairy. Undeterred, he presses into action what he proudly considers to be his histrionic ability and rearranges his rugged features into a simpering smile that is an amalgam of 'coyness and imbecility'. Dressed like an overblown daffodil but distinctly un-flower-or-fairy-like, he *does* tread the boards, with hilariously anarchic results.

By one of those astonishing coincidences which abound in the William books, Mr and Mrs Brown are in the audience. She is aghast at the spectacle of the bizarrely unethereal being on the

WILLIAM LOOKED AT FAIRY BLUEBELL HAUGHTILY. "IT'S NOT MY TURN," HE HISSED. "I'VE JUST SPOKE."

stage, who gruffly says his lines and then sits on a stool, lifting his butter muslin dress, taking nuts from the pocket of his muddy trousers underneath and cracking them 'with much facial contortion and bared teeth'. Mr Brown is equally shocked – but rapidly rallies by saying 'wildly', 'Who's William? There isn't any William. Temporarily I've disowned him.' It is left to the gym mistress, the art teacher and a horde of hysterical schoolgirls to exact retribution . . .

William's attitudes towards members of the fair sex are well defined in the early books. On the whole he has little time for them. As Richmal Crompton was to write much later (in the 1962 *Collectors' Digest Annual*): 'He dislikes little girls, not only because he considers them to belong to an inferior order of being but also because he suspects them of being allies of the civilization that threatens his liberty.' (Throughout the saga he makes no secret of his contempt for civilization. His classic quote is: 'I don't WANT to behave like a civilized yuman bein'. I'd rather be a savage any day. I bet savages don't let themselves be dragged off to dotty ole women when they'd rather go to see blood-curdlin' an' nerve-shatterin' westerns.')

The fearful feminine threat to William's freedom is expressed in his skirmishes with a variety of village stereotypes like Miss Milton, the

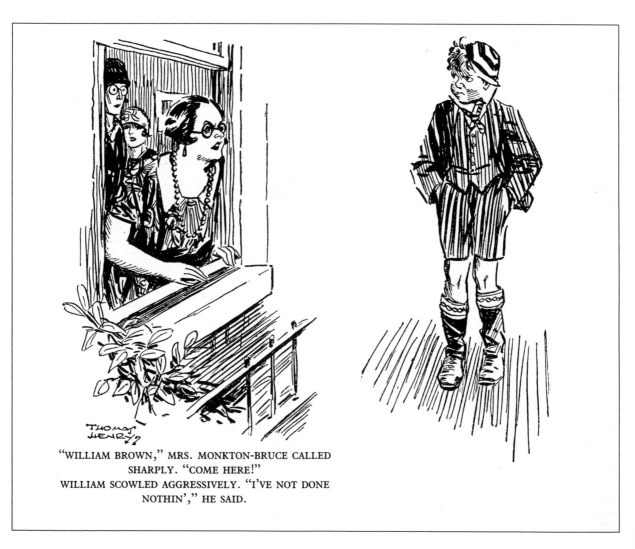

"WILLIAM BROWN," MRS. MONKTON-BRUCE CALLED SHARPLY. "COME HERE!"
WILLIAM SCOWLED AGGRESSIVELY. "I'VE NOT DONE NOTHIN'," HE SAID.

astringent martinet, and Mrs Monks, the vicar's wife, who, after having so many church functions wrecked by the Outlaws, feels fully justified in foiling their knavish tricks. There are also those solemn ladies who are concerned with Higher Thought or Perfect Love or Psychic Phenomena whose doings both intrigue and repel William. Generally speaking, these female seekers of truth or appreciators of art are not over-responsive to the male sex. As Miss Featherstone of the Literary Society nervously predicts, 'as soon as you begin to have men in a thing it complicates it at once'. However, in *William – the Good* the society's Secretary, Mrs Bruce Monkton-Bruce, co-opts William to help backstage with sound- and other effects when they decide to put on a historical play called *A Trial of Love*. The literary ladies realize how useful his 'noises off' might be when they first hear his frightful whistle, which is evocative of the howling winds that are atmospherically essential to their production. William, of course, thinks that he is the most important 'actor' of them all and goes over the top on the first night, creating a truly deafening and almost endless storm, throwing squibs around during passages of serious dialogue to remind the audience that the war between the Cavaliers and Roundheads is still being waged, and bringing the action to a climax when (through ignorance rather than intention) he empties the contents of a bucket of water over the heroine's head (instead of the tiny pieces of torn-up paper which, stored in another bucket, are supposed to represent falling snow). On the whole William can cope fairly well with the most determined of elderly or middle-aged females. The direst threat to his noble (or ignoble) savage state comes in the form of that frill-bedecked, diminutive bundle of pertness that is Violet Elizabeth, the darling only child of the stinkingly rich sauce magnate who lives with his family at the Hall.

William's first meeting with Violet Elizabeth in *Still – William* is a classic example of the clash between the sexes. 'William, pirate and Red Indian and desperado, William, woman-hater and girl-despiser' finds his worst fears about girlish ghastliness realized when he is forced by his mother to go to tea at the Botts' and meet the lisping little horror. She has bubbly blonde curls, glowing like a golden halo, a squeaky-clean pink and white face and a filmy white lacy frock, from the ballet-type skirts of which peep white silk-socked legs and white buckskin shoes.

She shamelessly imposes her will upon him by threatening tears (the famous threat to 'thcream and thcream' until she's 'thick' comes a little later). For William there is no escape from her tear-filling eyes and trembling lips as she insists that he plays 'little girlth gameth'

"NOW YOU MUTH PLAY WITH ME," LISPED VIOLET ELIZABETH, SWEETLY.
"I DON'T PLAY LITTLE GIRL'S GAMES," ANSWERED THE DISGUSTED WILLIAM.

STILL ——
WILLIAM
RICHMAL CROMPTON

THE MOST POPULAR *William* BOY IN FICTION

JUST HIS LUCK!

with her, that he really likes 'all little girlth' and – most humiliating and horrific of all – that he wishes he *was* a little girl.

> 'Er – yes. Honest I do,' said the unhappy William.
> 'Kith me,' she said raising her glowing face.
> William was broken.
> He brushed her cheek with his.

But even worse torture is to follow that notorious kiss as she piles on the final indignity: 'Now leth play fairieth. I'll thow you how.' He spends the rest of the afternoon agonizingly, 'in the character of a gnome attending upon Violet Elizabeth in the character of the fairy queen.'

The only female influence in William's life which he welcomes in a fairly sustained way is that of Joan, the unshowy, quiet and amiable girl who lives (at least early on in the saga) next door. She is the only female member of the Outlaws but makes few psychological demands on them, happily accepting submissive roles in all their games (she is, for example, an ideal Red Indian squaw). She sees William always as a 'god-like hero' whose 'very wickedness partook of the divine . . .' In *Still – William* he pays her the greatest compliment in his repertoire (when he is on the rebound from a crush on Miss Dobson, the Sunday School teacher's pretty sister, whom Robert also fancies and whose Valentine of a big box of chocolates she much prefers to William's home-made one of battered cardboard and gluey wilting leaves):

> '. . . I like you better than *any* insect, Joan,' he said generously.
> 'Oh, William, do you really?' said Joan, deeply touched.

He is often very protective of her, and of other small girls who have dark hair and dimples which remind him of her. It seems unlikely, however, that she is the 'little girl next door' in that first published story 'Rice Mould', which is reprinted in *More – William*, because the exploit ends with her look of ecstasy

"*MONEY* DON'T MATTER," SAID WILLIAM. "THINGS IS CHEAP TO-DAY. AWFUL CHEAP!"

(when she thinks she is about to taste cream blancmange) turning to one of fury when she realizes that William has brought her the hated rice-mould by mistake; one cannot imagine the adoring Joan ever being furious with William.

William's endeavour to provide her with the delicacy for which she yearns fits into his image of himself as the strong, generous, all-providing male. Only a few females stir him to play this role. One little girl who does so in *Just – William* is fortunate to encounter him when he is temporarily in charge of the village sweet-shop because of the enforced absence of its owner, Mr Moss. She has only four pennies to spend but, moved by her golden curls, blue eyes, velvety and rosy cheeks, William loads her with as many sweets as she can carry, revels in bestowing such lordly bounty and, when she kisses her hand

WILLIAM AND JOAN DO THEIR BEST TO KEEP THE CHRISTMAS PARTY GOING ALL NIGHT

④ WITH JOANS HELP, WILLIAM HIDES THE HATS AND COATS OF THE GUESTS

⑤ WILLIAM, THE OPPORTUNIST, RELIEVES HIS BROTHER ROBERT OF HIS WATCH

⑥ THEN WILLIAM AND JOAN GO BACK AND AMUSE THE PARTY.

⑦ BUT UNFORTUNATELY WILLIAM'S REPERTOIRE NEVER VERY EXTENSIVE, GIVES OUT SUDDENLY AND WHEN HE IS COMPELLED TO FALL BACK ON "THE WRECK OF THE HESPERUS," THE BREAK-UP OF THE PARTY COMMENCES IMMEDIATELY in goodbye to him, blinks 'with pure emotion.'

In *Just – William* another female inspires his (short-lived) adulation. His long-suffering and attractive teacher, Miss Drew, despairing of making him understand a simple mathematical problem, tells him to stay in after school for further explanations. It is then that, while she bends over her desk, the sun streams through the window and illuminates the golden curls in the nape of her neck: 'There was a faint perfume about her, and William the devil-may-care-pirate and robber-chief, the stern despiser of all things effeminate, felt the first dart of the malicious blind god.' Desperate to please her, he insists that he now 'unnerstands' the problem with which they have been grappling. (He

WILLIAM FELT THE FIRST DART OF THE LITTLE BLIND
GOD. HE BLUSHED AND SIMPERED.

doesn't, of course!) She wearily suggests that he'd have done so more quickly if he hadn't played with dead lizards all the time when he should have been concentrating in class, and he presumably accepts the criticism because he goes home 'her devoted slave'. The next day he cuts every flower from his father's greenhouse to present to her: later he puts so much energy into his homework that Mr Brown gathers up his newspaper and quietly creeps away from him to the veranda 'where his wife sat with the week's mending'. He tells her that 'William's gone raving mad ... Takes the form of a wild thirst for knowledge, and a babbling of a Miss Drawing, or Drew, or something ...' Fortunately for himself, for his family and indeed for his teacher, William soon gets over his infatuation.

His attitudes not only to girls but to school, holidays, church, cats, dogs, entertainments and many aspects of his world are defined in the books of the 1920s. His exploits during this decade also bring him into relationships with several examples of the perfect – or perfectly awful and spoilt – boy. He is even more contemptuous of these than he is of girls. Hubert Lane is, of course, a prime example but at least he offers William the satisfaction of being a long-term enemy on whom he can, figuratively, sharpen his teeth. The worst mummy's-little-masculine-darlings are hangovers from the Victorian era who wear sailor, velvet or Kate Greenaway suits. A surprising number of these small boys crop up in William's village. There is Cuthbert in *More – William*, a cousin of Joan who seems briefly to be replacing William in her affections. He is garbed in an embroidered tunic, 'very short knickers and white socks', has a golden halo of curls, doesn't like William's 'rough gameth' and suggests that they 'thit down' and tell 'fairy storieth' instead. William eventually gets the better of him when, in a production of *Red Riding Hood*, he – in the role of the wolf – almost savages the prissy paragon. William is condemned by most of the audience – but Joan is stirred by his dominating performance to tell him how much she loves him because he does 'such 'citing things!'

Then there is Bertie in *William – the Outlaw*, the nephew of William's headmaster who is temporarily in William's class at school. His 'beautiful conscience' forces him to tell tales to his uncle about William's misdeeds. When the grown-ups arrange a pageant, sweet little Bertie is the only child they trust to take part but, manipulating Bertie through his unbounded conceit, William contrives to remove him from the role of page to Queen Elizabeth I. He plays this himself – to the enthusiastic cheers of his schoolmates who, coerced into watching the pageant, have been expecting to see the odious Bertie hogging the limelight.

Of the many 'cissies' who cross William's path during the decade, Georgie Murdoch is the most flagrant – and his come-uppance is the most satisfying. His 'perfection' makes the Outlaws' lives a misery. Their mothers constantly hold him up as an example to them, and the white-suited, smarmy, tale-bearing, impeccably mannered Georgie gets 'sickniner an' sickniner' by the day. Eventually William's position as the leader of the Outlaws is in jeopardy unless he can find a way to put down the obnoxious Georgie.

William seizes his opportunity when, at a garden party, the children are asked to present scenes from British history. He suggests enacting an episode from the life of King John *after* he 'loses his things in the Wash'. Georgie agrees so long as he can be the King; his weakness is that he will never admit his ignorance about anything, so he has to accept the gems of historical misinformation which William feeds to him. He allows William, in the interests of authenticity, *slightly* to muddy his perfect person and sailor suit, but William smothers him with evil-smelling mud and tells him that the names of his two courtiers are 'Dam and Blarst'. When the unusually filthy Georgie, in the belief that he is correctly addressing his minions, declaims 'Oh, Dam and Blarst' in front of a shocked audience, his days in the village are numbered. His erstwhile

"MY COUSIN'S OFFERED A BOX OF CHOCOLATE CREAMS AS A PRIZE TO THE ONE WHO ACTS BEST," MRS. MURDOCH WAS SAYING. GEORGIE'S EYES GLEAMED.

adult admirers cannot overlook 'the memory of that mud-caked little horror uttering horrible oaths'. Georgie and his family simply have to go – and to go quickly. William, once again, has salvaged his honour, and his right to leadership.

As Thomas Henry's wonderfully expressive pictures indicate, William has a vulnerable look during the 1920s, seeming almost tiny by the side of several grown-ups (particularly the Browns' formidable cook). Nevertheless he spends a lot of his time putting down pompous adults (often quite innocently). There is his encounter with Sir Giles Hampton in *William – the Good*, when this distinguished Thespian comes to recuperate in the village after a nervous breakdown. Set in the mould of larger-than-life Shakespearian

actor-managers of the period, Sir Giles asks William 'majestically' when the boy has collided with him if he knows who he is:

> 'No,' said William simply, 'an' I bet you don't know who I am either.'
> 'I'm a very great actor,' said the man.
> 'So'm I,' said William promptly.

This is at the time when William is working on his sound-effects for the Literary Society's production of *A Trial of Love*. Sir Giles, apparently, is so impressed by his repartee – and the hilarity which he injects into the play when it is produced – that he turns up trumps, donating a new football to William and the cinematograph to the Literary Society that they have wanted for some time but have been unable to afford.

In *William – the Fourth*, too, there is a fairly happy outcome to William's encounter with his self-important god-mother, the affluent Mrs Adolphus Crane, whom he eventually meets for the first time after his mother sends her a (presumably retouched) studio portrait of himself and she wants to see him. Scrubbed and polished to the point of discomfort and indignity, William finds himself 'trapped in a huge and horrible drawing-room by a huge and horrible woman'. Mrs Adolphus Crane's other guests begin to arrive, so she hands him her album of family photographs to occupy him until she is free to give him her illustrious attention. He relieves his boredom and irritation by drawing embellishments to his godmother's photographs which transform them from dignified portraits to grotesque cartoons. His artistic efforts are much appreciated by the other guests, who also have the photo album foisted on them by their self-satisfied hostess. She can't understand why her guests seem so lively and happy and (fortunately not bothering to look again into her albums) is convinced (in a way, accurately) that it is William who has made the party go with such a swing.

His most celebrated skirmish with a pompous adult during this period (in *Still – William*) takes place when he

"'E'S EAT NEARLY EVERYTHING, MUM."

"YOU CAN LOOK AT THE ALBUM WHILE I AM GETTING READY." WILLIAM WAS TRAPPED, TRAPPED IN A HUGE AND HORRIBLE DRAWING-ROOM, BY A HUGE AND HORRIBLE WOMAN.

WILLIAM—THE BAD

RICHMAL CROMPTON

"Oh, Crumbs!"

meets Lady Atkinson, who erupts into his life while he is resolutely experiencing a 'truthful Christmas' inspired (unusually) by the vicar's recent sermon on the necessity of abandoning 'all deceit and hypocrisy'. He is staying with his family at the home of his Uncle Frederick and Aunt Emma and has already alienated everyone by telling them – without the usual white lies that make for social harmony – that he doesn't like their (very boring) gifts to him. He also truthfully explains that his presents to his aunt and uncle (a pincushion and a leather purse) are not deserving of their expressed gratitude because they are hand-ons; the pincushion is faded and the purse has a faulty catch.

Lady Atkinson sails regally in to bestow her gift on Aunt Emma and Uncle Frederick. It is a photograph of herself. The adult members of William's family try to overcome the tense atmosphere that he has generated and make highly flattering remarks about her picture – which she smugly soaks up. She then asks the 'little boy' what he thinks of it. William, who is nothing if not resolute, then provides his 'final offering at the altar of truth' by telling the aristocratic personage that the photograph 'isn't as fat as you are . . . an' it's not got as many little lines on its face' and that it is prettier than its subject is in the flesh. Everyone, including Lady Atkinson, is outraged, and Aunt Emma collapses because she fears that her relationship with them is at an end. William's truthfulness, however, is rewarded: Uncle Frederick, who deeply dislikes the patronizing Lady Atkinson, slips William a half-crown . . .

William has a way of becoming involved with many colourful personalities who are very much of their period. For example, in *William – the Bad* he becomes the front legs of the dragon in a Merrie England pageant arranged by a Ruskinite couple, Adolphus and Euphemia Pennyman, who try to bring the village back to 'the simple life' and 'the morning of the world' by getting them to wear hand-woven smocks, eat nut cutlets instead of meat and do country-dancing rather than the Charleston and the Blues. (At the performance William fights within the dragon-skin with its back legs – the Pennymans' prissy nephew Pelleas, who wears Greenaway suits and doesn't like William because he is 'ugly – and chases St George (Adolphus) all over the place instead of allowing himself to be slaughtered by him.) William also becomes fascinated by the antics of members of the Society of Ancient Souls in *More – William*, and saves his friend, the mild Mr Gregorius Lambkin, from the matrimonial clutches of Miss Gregoria Mush; they are both believers in reincarnation and their practice of garbing themselves in Roman togas, etc. enables William to dupe Gregoria on April Fool's Day so humiliatingly that she leaves his friend well alone afterwards.

In *William – the Good* he innovatively uses one of the popular props of the period – a wireless set – to get rid of Uncle Frederick, who has come for a visit of unspecified length, bores the Brown family with endless, obsessive and detailed prattle about his marvellous stamp collection, and won't leave Robert alone for a moment with the current object of his affections – who is also staying at William's home. Our hero uses the marvels of modern science to put out a phoney S.O.S. message calling Uncle Frederick away because his stamp collection has been stolen . . .

WILLIAM -
THE DICTATOR

RICHMAL CROMPTON

THE MOST POPULAR *William* BOY IN FICTION

The 1930s – William the Leader

In the William saga the 1920s edge into the 1930s without any signs of dramatic change in either William's personal situation or in the life of the village. In fact, this apparent stability and changelessness was a reflection of the country at large at the beginning of the decade. By its end, however, we can sense various alterations of status, new social trends, and echoes of political and military challenges which were already disastrously affecting several European countries, and to which Britain could no longer turn a deaf ear. The massive increase in unemployment and the subsequent hunger-marches of the 1930s Depression are not featured directly in the William books, but some of their effects (greater concern with pensions and benefits, emphasis on inexpensive, outdoor walking- and camping-holidays, campaigns for better housing for the downtrodden who might otherwise become militant, and so on) add vigour and atmosphere to several of William's exploits. Many social distinctions were still meticulously observed, but as the decade progressed a more democratic spirit began generally to infiltrate the barriers of class (the levelling influences of 'the wireless', films and the early days of television probably helped to bring this about).

William – the Dictator (1938) illustrates the growth of democracy in William's village by focusing on the role of one of his main critics and antagonists, the formidably acerbic, skinny and vociferous Arabella Simpkin, who so often disrupts the Outlaws' shows and exhibitions by informing all and sundry that these are not worth the admission charge of a penny or a halfpenny which William and Co. are demanding:

> Arabella Simpkin, as usual, was the chief agitator. Arabella's mother earned her living by 'obliging' the ladies of the neighbourhood, but the social boundaries were very sketchy among the junior inhabitants of the village, and Arabella, by means of a forceful personality . . . dominated them . . .

The Brown family's domestic arrangements are also beginning to be brought

"WHAT HAVE I GOT FOR THE HALFPENNY I PAID?" SHE DEMANDED. "I'M NOT GOIN' TO PAY FOR A DRINK OF THAT OLE STUFF."

"EXPECTIN' ANYONE TO LIVE ON THAT!" SAID WILLIAM.
"DRY BREAD, SAME AS WHAT THEY GIVE TO PEOPLE IN
DUNGEONS!"

ing slowly from the spacious residence that it was during the 1920s. Then it was equipped with, as well as the usual living and bedrooms, a study, a library and numerous outbuildings such as sheds, stables and a summerhouse. By the end of the 1930s it appears to have become a solid but unpretentious detached house (and, by the late 50s, a smaller, semi-detached residence).

Unlike his house ('The Hollies'), William appears to grow bigger with the passage of the years. He is, of course, still eleven years old but Thomas Henry's illustrations suggest that he has become both physically larger and more self-assured than he was during the 20s. There is, for example, a marked contrast in his size between the pictures of him with the cook in *Just – William* (see page 33) and with Ellen in *William's Happy Days* (1930). Richmal's lively word pictures of William were perfectly matched by Thomas Henry's exuberant illustrations, in which, during the 30s, he was able to project with panache the whole range of William's facial expressions (from gloom to glee, from happy expectation to heavy apprehension, from outrage to unctuousness, etc.) as well as the flamboyant gestures of his body language.

William's role has become more closely entangled with that of his Outlaws than before, and his position as their leader has become consolidated at every level. He is not only a man of action, ferocious determination and imaginative enterprise, but an aspiring world-potentate whom we see in *William – the Pirate* (1932) reflecting on his regal powers and vast domain:

into line with the modern world. At a time when it was still commonplace for comfortably-off families to have at least one maid of all work, William's ménage includes a cook as well as the resident maid, Ellen or Emma (both names are used in the early stories and appear to be interchangeable). During the 30s, however, the gardener seems less in evidence and has presumably been relegated from full- to part-time employment. To counterbalance this economy a charwoman, Mrs Hobbin(s), begins to crop up in the stories from *William – the Rebel* (1933). Eventually she – or rather her successor in the job, Mrs Peters – becomes the Browns' only domestic help – but that is a long, post-war way off. Even though William's family resolutely hang on to their maid-cook-and-gardener status during the 30s, there is the suggestion that their house is shrink-

William sat on the crest of the hill, a small squat untidy figure, his chin cupped in his hands. From his point of vantage he surveyed the wide expanse of country that swept out before him, and as he surveyed it he became the owner of all the land and houses as far as he could see. Farther than he could see. Casting aside the hampering bonds of possibility as well as probability, he became the ruler of all England. Finding the confines even of England too cramping for him, he became the ruler of the whole world.

His imagination then whirls him into fantasies of sending his minions on life-or-death adventures to the farthest ends of the earth, of quelling violent revolutions, executing the rebels and pinning medals on to the breasts of his victorious generals. He is nothing if not wholesale in his visionary exploits, and generally speaking Ginger, Henry and Douglas are assigned quintessential roles in these. They have now become an extremely closely-bound group even though, jostling and shoving each other both figuratively and physically, they never overtly express their mutual affection.

Solidarity is taken for granted even when William the leader makes decisions which the others think are questionable. In *William – the Dictator* (1938) one story (which in the *Happy Mag* was eponymous but which changed in the book to 'What's in a Name?') shows the Outlaws as the Green shirts (inspired loosely by the blackshirt and brownshirt uniforms of the British Union of Fascists and the German Nazi party). Hubert Lane immediately copies them and forms his own band of followers into the Blue shirts; he, like William, is the dictator of his party and, stimulated by hearing his father say that 'all these shirt people want col'nies', he has inveigled an affluent aunt into letting the Laneites use her garden as the extra 'living space' which real-life dictators in Germany and Italy were at that time demanding. William boasts that his Green shirts have a far better colony which provides wonderful food as well as adventure and play opportunities, but Hubert guesses he is bluffing and makes a pact that, if William's colony is as good as he says it is, then the Blue shirts will surrender to the Outlaws. If it is not, and if Hubert's colony lives up to its description, William's Green shirts have to surrender to the Laneites. An inspection time of 6 p.m. that day is set, and Ginger, Henry and Douglas gloomily and bitterly round on William for what they see as his incompetence and

stupidity: '"Look what you've let us in for!" said Ginger', and '"It'll be jolly nice havin' to s'render to them,"' said Douglas' sardonically. But none of his friends dreams of separating himself from the group. (Needless to say, William's Micawber-like hope that something will turn up to rescue them from this predicament is more than fulfilled, and the episode ends with Hubert and his band, crestfallen, having to surrender to William and the Outlaws.)

The solidarity of the celebrated foursome is enhanced by their awareness that it is propitious to maintain a low profile about their activities as far as their families are concerned. Adult interference is likely to prevent their enterprises, so the Outlaws have, perceptively, opted to remain a secret society: 'In their shrinking from the glare of publicity they showed an example of unaffected modesty that many other public societies might profitably emulate.' By the 1930s Richmal Crompton is making splendid use of the childhood group or gang, conveying the authentic atmosphere of its friendships and rivalries, aspirations and allegiances. William carries his small-boy band through all vicissitudes with his sweeping optimism, wild imagination and dogged assertiveness. Yet, during this period, we do catch glimpses of William's awareness of his own limitations. (This is, perhaps consciously, balanced by his greater facility in the 30s than in the 20s for organizing iconoclastic fates for his enemies and antagonists rather than simply bringing these about through innocence and naïvety. His well-planned and long-sustained vengeance on his nastiest neighbour of all, the unnamed 'gorilla' in *William – the Pirate*, exemplifies this. William systematically drives him to distraction by making his doorbells ring repeatedly through a primitive but effective form of remote control.)

In *William – the Rebel* he is feeling despondent about having lived 'all these years and not *done* anything yet'. His mother points out that he's done quite enough, breaking every window in the house at one time or another, making the geyser explode twice, ruining the parquet floor by sliding on it and getting tar all over the hall carpet. Robert assures him that the world *will* ring with his name one day – 'I bet you any money we'll all live to see you hanged' – and Mrs Bott, calling at this inauspicious moment, tells Mrs Brown that William looks bilious and needs a dose of Gregory powder. He resignedly accepts this adult lack of sympathy and, more and more resentful at being 'eleven years old . . . and not done a *thing* with my life but sums an' g'ography an' stuff like that' he runs away from home – and even away from his beloved Outlaws (he does, of course, take Jumble with him). His feeling that he is a failure is short-lived because, discovering the over-weight Mr Bott trying to reduce in a Nature-Cure clinic where he is being pushed and pummelled about (massaged) and starved (drastically dieted), he alerts Mrs Bott, who 'rescues' her by now dispirited but still stout and saggy spouse and gratefully tells William that he has saved Botty's life. William, feeling that he will be able to capitalize on Mrs Bott's gratitude, is then buoyant enough to return home.

He actually lets the Outlaws down briefly in *William's Happy Days* when another of those cissy boys who seem to dog them turns up at their school. Reggie, 'dressed in a white sailor suit [with] a white sailor's cap perched on a riot of [curly] golden hair', seems more than ripe for ragging but he has an inbuilt streak of nasty tricks and know-how which protects him from the justifi-able wrath of his schoolmates. It is left to the Outlaws to find a way of putting down his cheek and cutting off his offending curls, but William by chance meets Reggie's sister Angela, whose dark hair and 'demure dimpled face' remind him of Joan (who departed from the village some time earlier), and when she begs him to look after her dear little brother he cannot resist: with her dark eyes fixed on him and her dimples 'coming and going anxiously' William was as 'Samson shorn of his locks'.

He cannot, of course, explain to the Outlaws that he has been seduced from his high purpose of paying Reggie out, and has to pretend that he's thinking up a master plan, during which time they should all be nice to Reggie to put him off his guard. Meanwhile Angela's little brother continues to behave sneakily and smugly; the Outlaws' patience with their leader nearly wears out, and Wil-liam has to fight several battles – with his own repulsion at his perfidious behaviour, with the fear that Angela will discover he hasn't the extraordinary influence over his schoolmasters that he claims ('"I jus' *look* at 'em," he said darkly . . . "it's a norful look"'), and with the apprehension that Ginger, Henry and Douglas will discover he is actually committed to protecting rather than punishing Reggie. Things seem likely to come to a head when he weakly pretends to Angela that he's persuaded Mr Ferris, the arithmetic master and temporary Head, to let Reggie off a detention (actually he hasn't even felt able to mention the subject to the teacher). He is reprieved at the eleventh hour by Angela's and Reggie's parents suddenly deciding to leave the district and go abroad: this means that his friends, though full of suspicion, never quite believe that he is reneging on them, and that Angela never realizes that William is not the boy of tremen-dous influence at school that she believes him to be. She makes his life tem-porarily bright with a touching farewell note ('I think that you are the most wonderful pursun in the wurld. I shal nevver forget you') which is balm to William's beleaguered psyche, but her appreciation of him has prompted her to ask Mr Ferris – whom she meets just before her family leave the village – exactly how it feels to be on the receiving end of William's 'norful' look and persuasive powers. Mr Ferris is too much of a sport to give William away to his ardent female admirer – but the out-come of William's boasts to Angela is his having to do an hour's extra arithmetic with him after school for a fortnight.

When yet another un-manly boy tan-gles with the Outlaws in *Sweet William* (1936), solidarity is the keynote. Ginger's Aunt Arabelle is looking after

WILLIAM— THE REBEL

Twelfth Impression

RICHMAL CROMPTON

"ALL RIGHT, YOU TRY TO MAKE ME DRINK IT," SHOUTED
ANTHONY MARTIN, "AND I'LL THROW IT IN YOUR NASTY
OLD FACE."

him during his parents' temporary absence, and all the Outlaws are anxious that he should receive the hoped-for generous tip which aunts often give at the end of their visits. (The Outlaws, of course, share all such tips.) They have unfortunately blotted their copybooks with her fairly early on, and realize that they have to bring off some sort of coup to get back into her good books. The answer rests not far away – in Honey-suckle Cottage, in fact, which has once again been let to temporary visitors – to Anthony Martin, his mother and his nurse. Anthony Martin is Richmal Crompton's side-swipe at Christopher Robin, A. A. Milne's besmocked and whimsical embodiment of childish charm, who appeared on the literary scene fairly soon after her own anti-hero was launched. Neat, squeaky clean and basically conformist, he is the anti-thesis of William. However, Richmal apparently loved Milne's *Now We are Six* because one of the poems in it had a metre taken from Horace, and she makes a graceful tribute to Christopher

Robin's saga in an earlier book, when William, Ginger and Douglas play a version of Pooh-sticks in the village stream.

In *Sweet William* her Christopher Robin *manqué* receives short shrift from the Outlaws. Anthony Martin brags to them that his well-known authoress mother features him and his pretty ways in '*literary* stories and poems' that appeal to 'really cultured people'. (These turn out to be clever send-ups by Richmal of the overwhelmingly popular 'Christopher Robin is Saying His Prayers' poem; each verse ends 'Anthony Martin is doing his sums' – or engaged in some other activity which echoes the rhythm of the Milne original: 'Anthony Martin is cleaning his teeth', 'Anthony Martin is milking a cow', etc.) Ginger's Aunt Arabelle lacks the literary fame of Anthony's devoted mamma, but yearns to interview the awesome and awful infant for a magazine called *Woman's Sphere*. However, the precocious Anthony and his pretentious parent refuse her request on the grounds that exposure in such 'a piffling paper . . . a twopenny-halfpenny rag . . . would cheapen our market'. Anthony fails to respond to the Outlaws' persuasive powers, partly through pique that they have never read any of his mother's books or poems about him, so William concocts and implements one of his master plans. They learn – when Anthony asks them to tea in order to show off to them – that far from being the charming child that his public image suggests, he is not only spoilt rotten but is a horrid little bully who gives his nurse a terrible time. William contrives secretly to record Anthony unleashing on that crushed-looking lady 'a torrent of invective which showed that, as far as mastery over words . . . was concerned, he had inherited much of his mother's literary talent'. The Outlaws play the record back to Anthony and, impervious to his stamping, biting, sobbing, kick-ing and scratching, blatantly blackmail him into giving Ginger's aunt the inter-view and being photographed sitting on her lap. He is forced to agree to protect his public image of juvenile sweetness and light. The Outlaws, of course, get the hoped-for ten-shilling tip.

Although this episode occurred in a 1930s book, it harks back to the literary scene of the 20s and, in fact, William is still grappling with many problems and situations which are reminiscent of the earlier decade. Ethel and Robert remain, in the words of a contemporaneous popular song – at least when they are between their various amours – 'fancy free and free for anything fancy'. Their behaviour towards William is, as ever, generally dismissive and unsatisfactory; there is little indication that their tolerance has matured as time has passed. William still tangles with a plethora of local clubs and societies which, if not perhaps so colourful as those of the 20s, still provide ample opportunity for the Outlaws' involvement in culture, politics and things psychic or philosophical ('she knows all about what a man called Froude said about dreams'). These societies of the 1930s include the Beekeepers' Guild, Children's Guild, Church Lads' Brigade, Educational Play Guild, Football Club, Amateur Dramatic Society, Literary Society, League of National Union, League of Perfect Health, League of Perfect Love, Marleigh Temperance Society, New Era Society, Open Air Holiday Association, Sick and Poor Fund and the Women's Institute. There are, in addition, the clubs and societies formed by the Outlaws themselves, which, despite their sometimes highly commendable objectives, are usually short-lived. Examples are their Society for Giving Decent Grown-Ups a Good Time and a Punishment Insurance Society, which for a premium of a penny a week offered its schoolboy members pay-outs of twopence for a detention and threepence for a caning. (It soon became 'bankrupt and discredited'.)

The ballroom dancing classes which William absolutely loathes have teetered on from the 20s to the 30s too, but after an incident in *William's Happy Days* in which he lets loose a dog in the girls' changing room with consequent devastation of stockings, gaiters and knickers, the teacher, Mrs Beauchamp, is so rude to Mrs Brown that she decides she won't allow William to attend any more of her dancing classes. This is an immense relief not only to him ('his heart was singing within him') but to lots of those little girls garbed in 'fairy-like frills and furbelows' who have constantly sidled up to Mrs Beauchamp pleading not to have to dance with William because he is 'so *awful*'.

There is the suggestion that Mrs Brown is very slightly altering her domesticated image, because, in *William – the Showman* (1937), she is helping every Wednesday afternoon at the Welfare Centre. From the same book we also learn that William's father is a freemason ('all they do is just dress up in little aprons an' whatnot'). As the 1930s advance, William is still unable to

"*NEED* I HAVE WILLIAM?" SHE PLEADED PITIFULLY. "HE'S SO *AWFUL*."

understand Mr Brown's ironic remarks; neither does he appreciate the deep concern with his education that has prompted his father to consider arranging regular individual coaching if William gets a poor school report: "'In the *holidays*," William exclaimed wildly. "... I'm sure there's *lors* against it ... I bet even *slaves* didn't have lessons in the holidays ... I shall only get ill with overworkin' an' get brain fever same as they do in books ...'" William goes on to inform Mr Brown that he'll not only have to pay doctors' and funeral bills for him, but also have to accept

some sort of retribution from a judge: 'His father, unmoved by this dark hint, replied, coolly, "I'm quite willing to risk it."'

This crisis in William's life is averted when he meets his Great Aunt Augusta on his way home from school with the report – which is, as usual, not one that will gladden his parents' hearts. This inept and bumbling lady has got lost on the way to the Browns' house; William leads her on tortuous paths through woods and fields, and nobly sacrifices his school report to make a trail of hundreds of tiny pieces of paper to ensure that they can find their way back if they take a wrong path. Aunt Augusta is profoundly impressed: 'I remember so well the joy and pride of the moment when I handed my school report to my parents. I'm sure you know that moment well.' William, of course, does not – but when they arrive home Mr Brown is so impressed by the miraculously good impression that his son has made on his 'only rich unmarried aunt' that though he's pretty sure of the report's execrable quality he decides to give William the benefit of the doubt. William's singing as he rushes off exultantly to meet the Outlaws can be heard a quarter of a mile away.

The pattern of fêtes, bazaars, sales of work and other village events continues, and William skirmishes at fairly frequent intervals with Miss Milton, General Moult and Mrs Bott, just as he did in the 20s. And there are no significant changes in the joys of the great outdoors: in *William – the Gangster* (1934) the Outlaws spend a typically enjoyable afternoon jostling and racing each other through the woods. They regret that they find no wild animals or previously unexplored territory, but rejoice in making a fire, damming a stream, climbing trees and being chased by a keeper. They still throw themselves into hedges and drag along in ditches – to the dire detriment of their clothing – as their mode of natural progression.

The 1930s bring William a new crop of heroes and role models but some old ones persist. In *William's Crowded Hours* (1931) the Outlaws come across a tramp

WILLIAM –
the GANGSTER

THE MOST POPULAR
William
BOY IN FICTION

RICHMAL CROMPTON

called Sandy Dick who is cooking over a smoky fire in the woods. Gentlemen of the road have always inspired them, so it is an easy matter for Sandy Dick to convince them that they can only become tramps when they grow up if they pay him, pretty well immediately, the necessary entrance fee to the profession of two shillings each. Thrilled at first, they soon find every attempt to raise this money abortive. Even the placid Mrs Brown, preoccupied as always with her darning, is outraged by William's requesting such a large sum. He assures her that it is for his future and that it will in the long run save his parents a lot of money, but she refuses to rise to the bait and says rather sternly that she doesn't believe in fortune-telling. Ethel is no more forthcoming, even though William offers the inducement that if she gives him two shillings she'll never see him again after he's twenty-one!

William's resourcefulness quickly comes to his aid. Ethel is now, we are told, in love for the very first time – with Jimmie Moore – and in consequence has thrown out a drawerful of photographs of her erstwhile admirers. William feels that people will pay money for photos, and he and the Outlaws set up a stand of packing cases for a White Elephant stall at the village's sale of work. No one is interested in buying Douglas's mutilated old prayer-book, Ginger's bird's nest and dead fern, Henry's broken-bottomed pail or William's spoutless teapot, bladeless razor (of Robert's) or newt in a jam jar.

Ethel's photographs, however, sell like the proverbial hot cakes. Each is inscribed with a loving and passionate message – so, of course, the youths who are escorting their current girl-friends around the sale of work are appalled to see their declarations of devotion to Ethel on view, and rush to buy them so that they can be destroyed before their new beloveds clap eyes upon them. Distraught young men throw down coins and pay the asking price several times over so that they can rapidly remove the offending pictures from the Outlaws' stall. 'Very thoughtfully William took his notice and altered "1d" to "1s".

"IF YOU'LL GIVE ME TWO SHILLINGS," SAID WILLIAM, "YOU'LL NEVER SEE ME AGAIN AFTER I'M TWENTY-ONE."

"CRUMBS!" SAID WILLIAM. "IT'LL PAY OUR ENTRANCE FEES AND MORE! AND ALL WITH OLD PHOTOGRAPHS!"

WILLIAM AND GINGER, THEIR MUSICAL INSTRUMENTS
AROUND THEM, LEAPT INTO A RIOT OF DISCORD.

Evidently the market value of old photographs was higher than he had supposed.' Their tramps' 'trade union dues' are quickly raised, but, felicitously, just as they are about to hand over their money to Sandy Dick, the police move in on him. The Outlaws settle instead for blowing their eight shillings on a lavish feast of lemonade and cream blodges (buns), and decide that scrumptious food in the hand is 'after all worth any amount of glorious careers in the bush'.

The fashions and mores of the 1930s influence William when he decides briefly on a career as a gangster, but this ambition is short-lived. He is up to the minute in dealing with supposed drug-traffickers, and in opening a nightclub in *William – the Gangster*. The Outlaws are now desperate to raise two shillings and sixpence, which Victor Jameson is asking for the sale of a splendid football. In response to Violet Elizabeth's suggestion ('My father knowth a man that made loth of money by night clubth') they convert the old barn into such an establishment, and William and Ginger

agree to be the essential orchestra. With William using a mouth-organ and a tin tray, and Ginger a trumpet and a particularly raucous rattle, they leap 'into a riot of discord worthy of the highest traditions of jazz'. Needless to say, in spite of all their and Henry's and Douglas's efforts, the youthful audience is not satisfied and is soon demanding its money back. However, Violet Elizabeth, who seems very well up in the night-life of the period, is determined that 'there muth be a raid ... by the polith' and accordingly informs the local force that there are suspicious goings-on in the old barn. The local constable appears and on investigation finds hidden there some sacks of loot from recent robberies in the neighbourhood. He is so delighted with his discovery that Violet Elizabeth quickly persuades him to donate half a crown to the Outlaws, who then get the football.

There are signs in *William's Crowded Hours* that William is softening drastically in the sternly masculine approach that he endeavours to adopt towards the opposite sex. He meets Hubert Lane's cousin, Dorinda, who surprisingly turns out to be as appealing as Hubert is repellent. William manages to establish himself as a hero in her eyes by chasing Farmer Jenks's bull, and then, by apparent use of magic, providing a lavish feast for her and Hubert (which is actually the range of entries for the Women's Guild's Cookery Exhibition). Dorinda is quite entranced by him and, when she raises her face and kisses him, he finds her 'unexpectedly pleasant to kiss'. It is perhaps as well for his girl-hating image that he has only one other encounter with the delightful Dorinda, in *William – the Pirate*, when her admiration for him continues to spill over.

She is staying once more with her aunt (Hubert's mother) and is to attend a performance of *Hamlet* at William's school. He has wisely been cast as a non-speaking attendant at the court of Elsinore, but decides that he must appropriate the star part in order to dazzle Dorinda. He mugs up on only one of Hamlet's monologues and, although his version of 'To be or not to be' is distinctly garbled, he relies on his wonderful powers of improvisation to get him through the play. He is not a bit deterred by the fact that another boy, Dalrymple, is the chosen Prince of Denmark; as soon as William can leap on to the stage he launches immediately into the celebrated words. His form-master's frantic attempts to get him back again into the wings result in his having to chase William round and round the stage. Shakespeare's illustrious tragedy is reduced to farce, which is much appreciated by Dorinda and most of the audience.

William's romantic impulses are stirred by another and a very different female in *William – the Pirate*. Robert rather grudgingly honours a promise to take his younger brother to a pantomime (and ostentatiously demonstrates his boredom with the whole business by reading Chekhov during the intervals), which wildly stirs William's imagination and delight. He laughs so hard at the comedians that he fears he may break a rib, he cheers and claps louder and longer than anyone else in the audience – and he falls in love with the heroine, Princess Goldilocks. For some days afterwards he spends a lot of time in a dream of wooing and winning her; seeming unusually quiet to his family, he is engaged in fantasies of fighting armies of brigands single-handed or killing ferocious beasts in order to rescue her. Soon, however, daydreams are not enough, and William decides to seek her out in the flesh and propose to her.

WILLIAM FELL IN LOVE WITH PRINCESS GOLDILOCKS. EVERY SMILE SHE THREW AT THE AUDIENCE THRILLED HIM.

AND SHE SEEMED TO SMILE DIRECTLY AT HIM, TO SPEAK TO HIM ALONE.

By one of those odd quirks of fate that so often recur in the William saga, Princess Goldilocks – or rather the actress who plays her role – is staying at a hotel in Marleigh. William goes through a series of bizarre adventures to get into her presence and when he eventually succeeds he makes an unceremonious entry into her room in a large laundry basket. As soon as she throws back the lid he becomes aware that she does not look quite as she did on the stage. She seems older and less sweet: in fact 'much older and much less sweet'. Instead of being the radiant young woman who has utterly charmed him, she seems at close quarters elderly and irritable. She – not unnaturally – is disturbed by his presence in the laundry basket and in her room, and angrily snaps at him. We are told that 'William was silent, returning her in imagination to the brigands and pirates and wild beasts from which he had in imagination so often rescued her'.

Someone who was to play a significant role in William's life came into the saga in *William's Happy Days*. He was to become part friend, part protégé, and part inspiration for the Outlaws. First mentioned as Tristram Mannister, and then, in *William – the Bold* (1950), as Tristram Archibald Mannister 'known to the whole neighbourhood as Archie', he appeared in nineteen of the stories, including one in the last book, *William the Lawless* (1970). In both Richmal's text and Thomas Henry's illustrations he has achieved startling transformation, mellowing from being the freakish twin brother of Auriole Mannister into an appealing though somewhat inept personality, and from a pale, bespectacled, skimpy-haired, apparently middle-aged man to someone much younger-looking with plentiful dark hair and a well-trimmed beard. In fact it seems likely that Thomas Henry had not realized when depicting them that the Tristram Mannister of *William's Happy Days* was the same character as the subsequent Archie (see illustrations on pages 49 and 75).

In the opinion of the Outlaws he is not just the usual 'loony' artist, although, like several of those whom they categorize as such, he first takes up temporary residence in the village – with his sister – in Honeysuckle Cottage, which seems to specialize in short lettings. Later in the stories he occupies a small 'tumbledown' house which is known as 'Archie's cottage'. He adheres to the 'aggressively modern' school of painting and his unintelligible abstracts bring him scant success. However, when pressed for cash he can employ more conventional styles and produce calendars and greetings cards which people are prepared to buy. In the 1950s and 60s he becomes established as the regular local artist and also as one of Ethel's long-term admirers, wildly idealizing her, lacking the kind of sophisticated charm which could attract her, but providing the faithful devotion on which she is occasionally prepared to fall back. Unlike her, the Outlaws find Archie and his bohemian life-style constantly intriguing: they are attracted to his chaotic domestic arrangements, his daubings and his slightly resigned but genial acceptance of their friendship. They feel extremely protective towards him, recognizing, if unable to name, the unworldliness that emanates from him.

In *William's Happy Days* he and Auriole are introduced as 'twins', the only difference in their appearance being that 'one [Archie] wore knickerbockers and the other [Auriole] a skirt'. Even the worsted stockings and brogues which are evident below the knickerbockers and skirt are identical, as are their pallid, lean faces, light Eton-cropped coiffures and homespun tweeds. William takes to the pair immediately, and they accept him almost as someone who goes with their rented cottage. It is only a few years since Sir Arthur Conan Doyle publicized the Cottingley fairy photographs which had vividly caught the public's imagination, and Auriole burns with ambition to snap a nature spirit. Her brother's aspiration is to paint other-worldly pictures, from psychic stimulation. William, quite accurately, sees these as meaningless and nightmarish, but he would like to help the Mannisters to achieve their ambitions if he could. It is in fact entirely due to him (though they do not realize this) that each achieves the ultimate fulfilment of having a picture published in the paper *Psychic Realms*. It is William, smothered inadvertently in grass cuttings, who is the subject of Auriole's photograph of what she thinks is a green nature spirit or fairy, and it is his painting of 'A Lion' that gets mixed up with Tristram Archibald's pictures and is chosen by 'an art expert' for reproduction as 'Vision' . . . 'a splendid example of inspirational painting'.

The Mannister twins are possibly the only adults on record to appreciate the Outlaws' famous brew – liquorice water. They have given up stimulants (tea, coffee and alcohol), which 'dull the psychic faculties', but realize that they must keep their other-worldly inspiration lubricated by some kind of liquid intake. They try some liquorice water, which William makes; in Auriole's opinion this is 'very nice . . . a pure herbal drink' and in her brother's 'quite delicious'. Their response does much to endear them to William, who has never before met 'a grown-up who did not look upon liquorice water as a messy juvenile concoction to be thrown away with contumacy whenever discovered'. Unlike Archie, Auriole plays no further part in the saga, although later stories mention that she has set up an Arts and Crafts Centre in the Lake District. The twins' elder sister, Euphemia, is also referred to.

Typical trappings of the 1930s crop up in the stories: in *William – the Rebel*, William is shown as collecting cigarette-cards (an immensely popular hobby with children of the period) and in the same book the widespread influence of 'the wireless' is evident. From the beginning of the saga, in the first chapter of *Just – William*, of course, cinematic influences have been at work. After William's visit to the pictures he upsets his father by knocking him into a rhododendron bush (William's clumsiness comes about because, emulating the hero of one of the films, he is escaping from imaginary pursuers), and he moves Joan to compassion by

MISS AURIOLE GAVE A SCREAM OF EXCITEMENT. "HERE IT IS! LOOK!" SHE EXCLAIMED.

implying that like one of the juvenile cinematic characters he will die very young. Naturally he is also inspired to sort out Ethel's romantic entanglements, with anarchic results, and he responds to his father's more vituperative than usual behaviour by wondering if, like the renegade in one of the films, Mr Brown could be a drunkard.

By the 1930s cinema-going was a regular activity with many families and its social repercussions were less extreme. In *William – the Rebel* it is obvious that members of Robert's set are romantically influenced by their film idols. Robert apparently is inclined to fancy every female film-star he sees on the silver screen, and subsequently every girl who remotely resembles them: he had, apparently, fallen in love with real-life Cornelia Gerrard 'because she reminded him of Greta Garbo', but soon after this he saw a picture starring Marlene Dietrich with the result 'that Cornelia was not his type, after all, but that Lorna Barton, whose profile really had a distinct look of Marlene Dietrich, was his true soul's mate'.

Similarly Cornelia has become disenchanted by Robert and cannot now understand how she ever thought that he looked like Ronald Colman. She cheerfully abandons him to become engaged to Peter Greenham, chiefly because he puts her in mind of Maurice Chevalier.

In *William – the Showman* (1937) William not only becomes involved with a film-star – Jimmie Minster, the famous juvenile lead – but at the young movie-actor's request impersonates him when he wants to go off and play at Red Indians with Ginger, Henry and Douglas and get out of attending a 'mayoral banquet' arranged by Hubert and Mrs Lane. (This is during a period when William & Co. set themselves up as their own 'Mare and Corprashen' and Hubert, in his usual copy-cat way, follows suit with his own gang.) Jimmie's agent felt that there would be good publicity value in the boy star's agreeing

to meet local children in this way – so of course William is delighted to be able to kill several birds with one stone. Heavily disguised in the costume of a masked cavalier which Jimmie wears in one of his films, he dupes Hubert and the Laneites; he enjoys a great and lavish meal, and relishes his role of film-star.

In the 30s there was a vogue for many types of outdoor exercise (which being mainly inexpensive was appropriate for those recessionary years). Long or short country rambles and hiking holidays were particularly popular – as indicated in 'I'm Happy When I'm Hiking', which was a best-selling song of the decade – and Thomas Henry exploited this trend by sending William on a walking holiday in one of his double-page *Happy Mag* cartoon spreads. Richmal brings him into contact with the participants in a camp organized by the Open Air Holiday Association in *William – the Detective* (1935). These energetic lovers of the great outdoors perform physical jerks, take long tramps over the hills, and play tennis and cricket. Their outfits typify the feeling of athletic freedom which clothes of the 1930s often conveyed: bright young females wear garments that vary from backless beach-pyjamas to flannel shorts, riding-breeches, cotton dresses and kitchen-type overalls. Stout ladies sport flowered cretonne beach-pyjamas, and the male campers wear shorts that reveal knobbly knees, or the kinder and less-revealing plus-fours.

William embraces a popular cause of the period – slum clearance – in *William – the Showman*. He is impressed by Miss Milton's impassioned plea to his mother that every family of 'ordinary means' should adopt a poor family – 'give them cast-off clothing, plants from the garden, food, financial assistance' and help to solve all their 'little problems . . . I want it to be a great social movement sweeping the whole of England.' Miss Milton goes on to say that she feels this will solve all the nation's social problems. For once the usually cooperative Mrs Brown shows surprising spirit in rejecting this appeal, pointing out that it's all her husband can do to support his

"THERE AREN'T ANY SHOPS HERE," COMPLAINED THE
GIRL IN THE BEACH PYJAMAS.

own family. Miss Milton takes her leave in 'majestic displeasure' and William, inspired by her rhetoric, follows her instructions to the letter. He takes a pocket full of crushed gingerbread and garden roots, plus one penny (his sole financial resource), to offer to the poor of Hadley. He goes even further, and in the spirit of her appeal decides to give love and security to a small urchin called Albert, and lasting emotional satisfaction to Miss Milton, by rehousing him in her home. He secretly transfers Albert to her bed (boots, grubby clothing, half-sucked toffee-apple and all) and, of course, activates a Williamesque chain of anarchic misunderstandings and mishaps. Miss Milton is certainly *not* amused!

In *Sweet William* he less altruistically takes up the issue of Pensions for Boys. He is outraged when he discovers that many adults receive an old-age pension of ten shillings a week (a fortune in his view) without having 'to do anythin'' at all for it', while boys who 'work all day long, goin' to school an' doin' sums and suchlike' get absolutely nothing except what niggardly pocket-money their parents might – or might not – dispense. The Outlaws' campaign for Pensions for Boys is strongly influenced by Henry, as an aunt of his had fought for the female vote by chaining herself to railings, making speeches from a lorry that toured the streets, and so on. William takes several leaves from the suffragettes' book in the matter of tactics – without marked success. The 'bomb' which the Outlaws plant in church makes such a pathetically feeble 'plup' that it is smothered by the vicar's resonant voice (this is not surprising, as their bomb consisted of the only readily available explosive they could find – a jaded-looking left-over Christmas cracker). They decide that they must march on London to put their position before the government, but on the way their campaign reaches its nadir when they meet and fall foul of the girls of Wentworth School, who resent the fact that this drive for juvenile pensions does not include female hand-outs. The Outlaws find themselves on the receiving

"THEY GET TEN SHILLINGS A WEEK FOR DOING NOTHING, WHILE WE WORK AN' WORK AN' WORK DAY AFTER DAY."

end of womanly militancy which smacks of the worst excesses of the suffragettes, as their bodies are attacked with hockey-sticks, rulers and geometrical compass points.

In several stories William becomes involved in politics, and he supports whichever party would be likely to hold power (so that he could, of course, be prime minister). He ventures beyond the confines of the Conservative, Liberal and Labour parties into Bolshevism at one extreme and Fascism at the other. As we have seen, he flirts with the props of totalitarianism in *William – the Dictator* by starting a Green shirt movement which is vaguely inspired by fascist brownshirt and blackshirt groups. He goes further in a story, 'William and the Nasties', which was first published in the *Happy Mag* in 1934 when perhaps there was not much awareness in Britain of the meaning of Nazism. The episode, reprinted in *William – the Detective*, appears to have been stimulated by some bilingual wordplay on the part of the Outlaws. They have been discussing the 'nasties' in Germany who, according to Henry, chase out Jews 'and take all the stuff they leave behind'. The implications of this are appealing when they recall that Mr Isaacs, who is Jewish and has taken over Mr Moss's sweet-shop, might be giving them short measure of liquorice ribbons, lollipops, etc. and that they could frighten him away and take over his stock. William declares in a business-like manner that they'd better start 'bein' nasties' straight away:

'I'll be the chief one. What's he called in Germany?'
'Herr Hitler,' said Henry.
'*Herr!*' echoed William in disgust. 'Is it a woman?'

To conform with his male-chauvinist precepts he announces that he will be 'Him' Hitler. Their initial efforts to ter-rorize Mr Isaacs fail, because their home-made swastika banner inspires fury rather than fear in his breast and instead of running away he chases them and boxes William's ears. They return after dark and, ironically, lock up in a small room a burglar whom they mistake for the sweet-shop owner. They then stumble on Mr Isaacs, who has been bound and gagged by the intruder. He is so grateful to them for releasing him that he says, 'Take vatever you vant. You can have as much as you can carry,' and they take this literally. This is the only time in the whole saga that the Outlaws engage in anti-Semitic exploits and, indeed, even before the episode has been satisfactorily resolved Richmal Crompton records that 'a strange distaste for the whole adventure' is beginning to engulf them. All's well

EVEN MR. ISAACS WAS SURPRISED AT THE AMOUNT HIS RESCUERS COULD CARRY.

GINGER COULD SCARCELY BE SEEN FOR BOTTLES OF PEAR-DROPS AND OTHER SWEETS, AND HENRY'S ARMS WERE COMPLETELY OCCUPIED.

that ends well: Mr Isaacs is transformed from a stingy baddie into a beaming good-guy and promises to look after their confectionery requirements generously in the future.

The mystery, of course, is how the liberal-minded Richmal came to create this story. She might not, at the time, have known of the worst aspects of Nazism but she knew enough to make Henry say 'They've got people called storm troops an' when these Jews don't run away they knock 'em about till they do.' It is in fact possible that she simply intended to highlight the perniciousness of fascism and that the story got out of hand, with a publication deadline which didn't allow her time to scrap it or make drastic revisions.

At any rate, when the Macmillan reprints began in the 1980s this story was omitted because of its unsuitability for children today. (It should be remembered that the William stories of this period were originally published in a periodical for adults.) Another episode, entitled 'William and the League of Perfect Love', was also dropped from the 1985 edition of *William – the Detective*. It is one in which William behaves with unfeeling callousness towards rats – which are as we know animals that he normally respects and even venerates. The discarded story features Jumble in a canine rat-killing competition in which William's 'frenzied yells' of encouragement and 'frantic joy' as his pet deals out death and destruction seem quite out of character. In fact the same book includes an exploit called 'William the Rat Lover', in which, infuriated by 'sentimentality' about birds which results in sanctuaries being set up for them, he decides to give his energies to protecting rats. He and the Outlaws have a Rat Week, when they release rodents from traps into a sanctuary which they have created where food and drink are put down for them. There is a happy result for William. Mrs Brown forces him to participate in a fancy dress competition at a Children's Animal Fête. The only available (borrowed) costume is an uninspiring, faded one which 'might represent anyone or anything from Mary

WILLIAM HATED THE WHOLE BUSINESS.

Queen of Scots' page to Nelson'. William's mother decides that with 'the addition of a bundle and the family cat it should represent Dick Whittington'. William is incensed at this, particularly because he knows that Hubert Lane, who has had a 'gorgeous' outfit specially made for the competition, is also going as Whittington. Nevertheless he sets out for the fête, under heavy parental pressure, clutching his mother's cat, Trouncer, who soon scratches his face and leaps out of his grasp like greased lighting. William then abandons his bundle and stick, trudges slowly to Marleigh Manor for the fête and, to his amazement, is chosen by Sir Gerald Markham as the winner and presented with the wonderful prize of a ciné camera. Sir Gerald, deploring the lack of originality in almost all the costumes, feels that only William has shown initiative and innovation. Unknown to him, as he walked past his rat sanctuary at the old barn, several of its denizens, hoping to be fed by him, slunk after him to Marleigh Manor. It is late afternoon and the light is conveniently murky: Sir Gerald awards William the prize for 'his excellent impersonation of the Pied Piper of Hamelin'. He comments that he doesn't know how he achieves his scenic effects (i.e. his rat retinue) but 'it was a clever idea brilliantly carried out . . .'

An interesting period touch in *William – the Detective* is its two separate references to the Loch Ness monster, which was then 'still well to the fore in the news'. A conversation about this elusive creature inspires 'in William's bosom an insatiable desire to capture a prehistoric monster'.

We cannot leave the 1930s without commenting that Ethel, sartorially, seems to have come into full glory in its fashionable, flowing dresses of flowered

NEW WILLIAM STORY
THE
HAPPY
SEPTEMBER
MAG.
7D

AN AMUSING INCIDENT FROM THE STORY "WILLIAM AND THE UNFAIR SEX"

chiffon, and elegant hairstyles. She seems to have grown younger in her appearance – though not of course in actual years – judging from Thomas Henry's attractive pictures of her during this period. Robert remains a student, but experiences the joys – and problems – of being promoted from motor-bike to car owner. Although in *William – the Pirate*, when he and Jameson Jameson are rivals for Emmeline Moston's affections, it can be an asset in the courting process, it sometimes has 'an irritating and incalculable way' of turning into a liability and temporarily giving up the ghost. His self-assurance takes a heavy knock when he and Emmeline have to take an unexpected four-mile walk home after a 'break-down' which turns out to be the result of an empty petrol-tank! In *William – the Gangster* his car has turned out to be so unreliable that William declares, when he and his brother are bound for a posh fancy dress dance at Hadley Grange: 'Well . . . I hope we aren't going in Robert's ole car.' They *are* of course, and it *does* break down – but the tortuous web of circumstances that William orchestrates as a result lead very indirectly to Robert saving his hostess's jewellery from being stolen – and becoming the hero of the hour.

In the second part of the decade, just before the shadows of future international conflicts began to produce widespread apprehension, the joyous and colourful coronation celebrations of King George VI and Queen Elizabeth lifted everyone's spirits. William and the Outlaws do full justice to this auspicious occasion in *William – the Showman*. The village holds its own Coronation Gala (with fancy dress once again the order of the day). Mrs Brown says that William can wear his Red Indian outfit but this time he yearns for something more regal to suit the event. He borrows without Robert's permission the kingly garb he had used in an amateur dramatic production of *King Cophetua and the Beggar Maid*. This puts Robert in a terrible position because, although he had planned to attend the gala in his other *School for Scandal* period costume, his current girl-friend, Dahlia Macnamara, tele-

WILLIAM TURNED TO THE VENGEFUL ROBERT.
"THIS IS MY BROTHER. HE VERY KINDLY LENT ME
HIS THINGS, ELSE I COULDN'T HAVE DONE IT."

ROBERT WAS SPEECHLESS WITH AMAZEMENT
AND INDIGNATION.

phones almost at the last minute to ask him to wear his royal outfit so that they can go as a pair (she representing the beggar-maid). This is really a sneaky ruse on her part: she wants to partner Robert's rival – Jameson Jameson – and makes this request to Robert so that he will not need his *School for Scandal* costume and will lend this to Jameson in response to his sudden request for it. Robert gladly loans the costume but then finds, to his horror, that the King Cophetua one has disappeared. He has to compromise with the very inferior costume which William had begun to make for himself before he decided to appropriate Robert's. This consists of a battered, gluey, gold-painted crown and an old, torn, red plush tablecloth.

Cursing his brother to high heaven, Robert is amazed to see that William has helped Mr Perkins the butcher to win the prize for the best float in the procession. Again, the villagers have been astoundingly unimaginative: their coronation floats are just like those they use on all special occasions except for a few bits of red, white and blue ribbon. Unknown to Mr Perkins, his float is adorned throughout the procession with the sparkling figure of William (in Robert's monarchial garb), squatting on a large potted palm in the butcher's truck. William graciously receives congratulations from the local M.P. and his wife. Robert, squirming with anger, can't wait to rip off his costume from William's back. He is, however, forestalled. William tells the M.P. that without his brother's kind loan of the costume he couldn't have become a prize-winner. He offers to change outfits with Robert – and the Member's daughter agrees to be shown around the gala's fair by Robert. She is, of course, 'the loveliest girl he'd ever seen in his life'.

William hurries through the merrymakers in search of his Outlaws. He has now become fed up with kings and coronations and, after a somewhat tiring afternoon, thinks he'll have 'a nice rest on the roundabouts or helter-skelter or wild sea waves'.

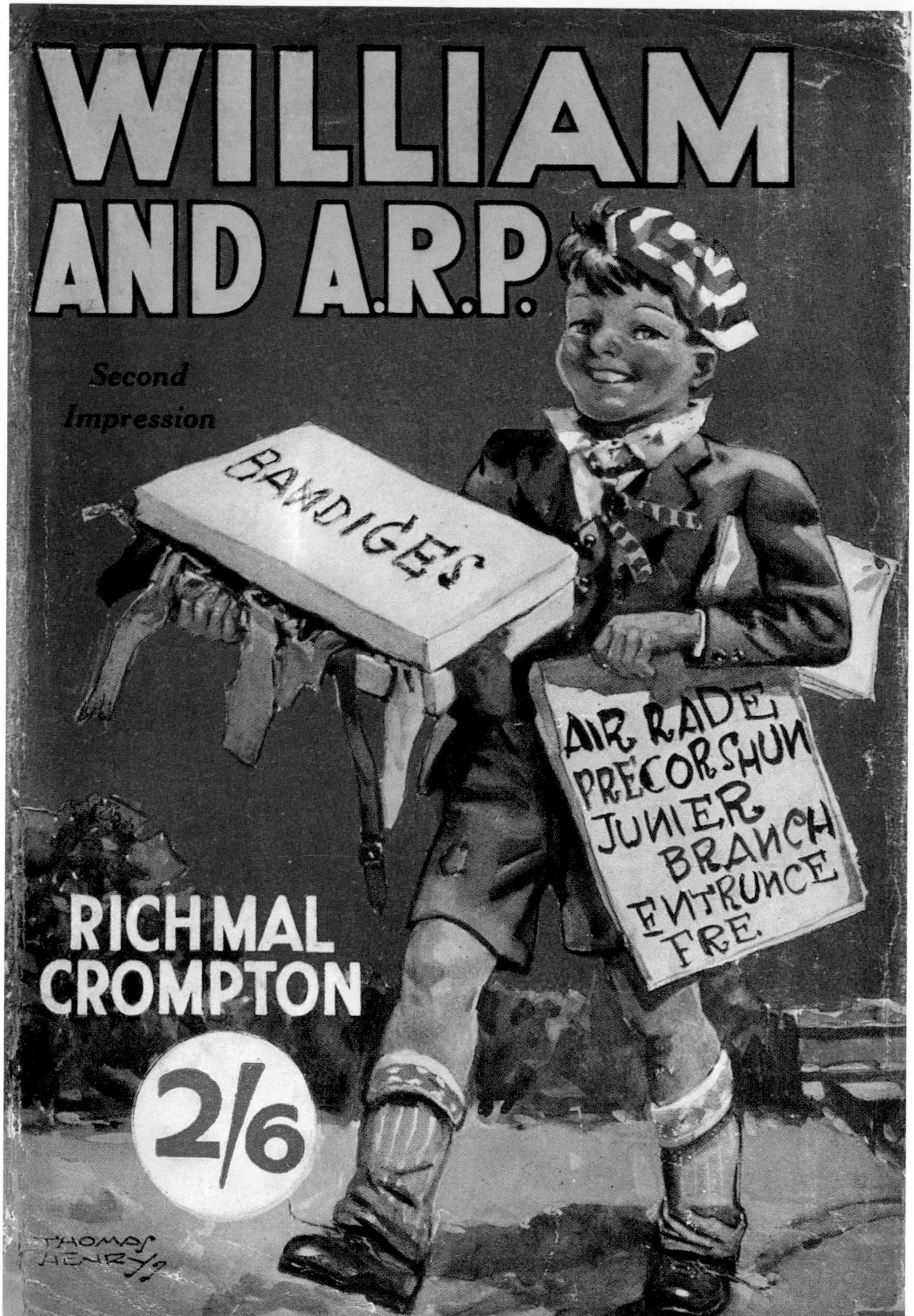
WILLIAM
AND A.R.P.
Second
Impression
BANDIGES
AIR RADE
PRECORSHUN
JUNIER
BRANCH
ENTRUNCE
FRE.
RICHMAL
CROMPTON
2/6
THOMAS
HENRY

The 1940s –
William at War

For William, as for so many real-life children, the nineteen-forties were dominated by the excitements, demands, challenges, restrictions and shake-ups of the Second World War. Although, as we have seen, social changes *did* take place during the 1920s and 30s, generally speaking the mood and tempo of life in and around William's village were untrammelled by dramas and disruptions (apart, of course, from those triggered off by William). After the outbreak of war in September 1939, the village, with its cottages, church hall, tidy shops and well-tended gardens, still nestled timelessly into its surrounding woods, meadows and hills, but the attitudes and activities of its residents were soon to find new outlets and expressions. In common with children everywhere else in Britain, William and the Outlaws were inspired to heights (and depths) of patriotic endeavour. They resolutely collected used comics and newspapers and old saucepans for salvage; they enthusiastically gathered shrapnel and fragments from shot-down aeroplanes for souvenirs and put on shows to raise money to buy Spitfires; they were frustrated but doggedly undeterred by shortages of sweets, favourite foods and toys; they helped – or tried to help – the Home Guard, Air Raid Wardens and Fire Fighters. Most of all they cherished fantasies of capturing Nazi spies.

William and A.R.P. was published in May 1939, during the post-Munich Agreement period of 'peace' which was in so many ways a preparation for the war which had become inevitable. The Spanish Civil War had made only too tragically evident the devastation that air-raids could inflict on combatants and non-combatants alike, and the British Government was getting a response to its request for civilian volunteers to train as air-raid wardens.

William loses no time in echoing the national mood. He and the Outlaws form their own AIR RADE PRE-CORSHUN, JUNIER BRANCH, and announce that for the first meeting it will be 'Entrunce Fre': ('They'll come if it's free,' said Douglas, with a tinge of bitterness in his voice. 'They always come to free things.') When William starts to tell his audience how to win the war, however, it is not wholly appreciative. Arabella Simpkin, 'a red-haired, sharp-featured maiden of domineering disposition', soon walks out in a huff because William has terrified her small, snivelling sister by threatening darkly that those who do not 'shut up an' listen' to him will be 'blown to bits by bombs and balloons and things'. The meeting's practical sessions (bandaging and trying on pseudo-gas masks made from flowerpots) proceed with rather more panache than William's lecture, though they do end in exhilarating free fights. In his mind, at least, the high-spot of the first A.R.P. meeting is the demonstration of 'decontamination' which Ginger suggests should take place at his house:

"LADIES AND GENTLEMEN," HE SHOUTED ABOVE THE UPROAR, "WILL YOU KINDLY SHUT UP AND LISTEN TO ME. I'M GOING TO TELL YOU HOW TO WIN THE WAR."

The cheers and uproar began again.

'... my mother's out ... an' the hose pipe's right at the bottom of the garden. I bet no one sees us ...' His optimism is unfounded, however. His mother arrives home soon after what William calls the 'detramination' business has begun, and witnesses 'the disgraceful scene – a wild medley of naked boys on the lawn, wrestling and leaping about in full play of the garden hose, manipulated by Ginger. Their clothes, which they had flung carelessly on the grass beside them, were soaked through ...'

William, thereafter painfully warned off by his parents from further participation in A.R.P., turns his attention to evacuation. He finds Hector and Herbert, seven-year-old twins, outside Hadley's leading toy shop and, deciding that they are suitable subjects for treatment, removes them to the 'safe area' of his village. He hides them temporarily in his family's cellar – with disastrous results. Hector and Herbert not only

pelt each other playfully with pickled eggs and potatoes from Mrs Brown's in-preparation-for-wartime-shortages-store, but hurl these and pieces of coal at William's mother and other ladies who enter the cellar to investigate the shouts of childish glee that emanate therefrom. For William the final irony occurs when Ethel and Robert, fresh from their (adult) A.R.P. class, seize one twin (who has a cut head) for bandaging practice and the other (who stinks from a bad egg missile) for a decontamination exercise.

As the war progresses, however, his enthusiasm and sometimes cock-eyed patriotism become fully restored and find intriguing forms of expression. Of course, he is not alone in this. Hard-working solidarity is the keynote in William's village, as it is everywhere else during the early 1940s. Many of the earnest ladies who had devoted their pre-war energies to societies for the promotion of Higher Thought, Total

Abstinence, Ancient Souls or Psychical Phenomena are now banded together as the Committee for the Entertainment of Evacuees (knitting and providing teas for the little darlings and horrors), the War Working Party (sewing for soldiers and helping in canteens) or as vegetable growers in gardens and allotments in the Dig For Victory campaign. Peppery ex-military gents, such as the Boer War veteran General Moult, and retired civil servants, applied their talents to the Home Guard or A.R.P. while deeply conservative farmers like the Outlaws' traditional enemy, Jenks, had to come to terms with shortages of manpower and accept the labour of land-girls (we remember Farmer Jenks's pretty helper Katie, the ally of William and his friends, who provided them with whatever additions she could find – including the glittering prize of a piece of a German bomb for their war trophies collection).

Most impressively, and very much in keeping with real-life responses, previously work-shy bright young things (perpetual students like Robert or play-girls like Ethel) surprised themselves and everybody else by joining up or taking on serious jobs in industry or as medical auxiliaries. Ethel in particular really comes into her own and incites even William's reluctant admiration for her contributions to the war effort. After two decades of simply going to parties and dances, looking decorative and attracting the admiration of an astounding variety of men, she goes to work with commendable vigour – in A.R.P., then the A.T.S. and as a nurse in a Voluntary Aid Detachment. Life on the Home Front for pleasure-loving females has, of course, changed enormously because of the exodus into the armed forces of all the village's able-bodied young men. There *are* potential swains for Ethel and her friends at the nearby R.A.F. station, but generally speaking the days of endless flirtation are – at least 'for the duration' – shelved. In *William and the Brains Trust* her younger brother takes pity on her when she is bored and deprived of companionship during one of her leaves from the A.T.S. He hits on the brilliant idea of getting Mr Polliter, his elderly relief history-master, to call and enliven one of Ethel's lonely evenings with his wonderful fund of stories and anecdotes. (Polliter is just about the only teacher who has ever been able to enthuse William for his subject.) It is all rather complex: Mr Polliter doesn't like accepting social engagements so William implies that his sister is retarded and in need of special coaching; she is terribly affronted when Mr Polliter appears, puts his hands on her celebrated red-gold curls and says kindly 'So here's little Ethel in her A.T.S. uniform.' (William has told him that she wears this garb as part of her delusionary process.) Happily, however, everything turns out well because a William-inspired misunderstanding brings Ethel into contact with Mr Polliter's son, a strapping and superbly good-looking army major who is also home on leave. Propinquity and chemistry ensure that the relationship flourishes for the appropriate period.

Robert's war effort proves equally worthy of William's admiration. He graduates from A.R.P. into the army and, when he becomes a second lieutenant in 'one of the less famous regiments', William resolves to make him into a hero. In *William Carries On* he boasts to Hubert Lane (with whom he is on temporarily good terms) about Robert's supposed derring-do: 'It was Robert who had conquered the Italians in Africa, raided the Lofoten Islands . . . who was solely responsible for the sinking of the *Bismarck* . . . It was Robert who had captured Rudolf Hess.' Hubert's credulity almost breaks down at this point and he points out that newspaper reports of the mysterious landing of Hitler's deputy in Scotland did not mention Robert, who, anyway, wasn't even there at the time. William's answer to this is simple: the truth has to be kept secret because his brother (despite his fairly lowly army rank) is so 'high-up' that his movements must never be revealed to the Germans. Tired of hearing Robert's praises so constantly sung, Hubert manages to upstage William by claiming that his mother's

second cousin Ronald has captured Hitler. In fact, Ronald has a friend, Lieutenant Orford, who, rather tickled by his resemblance to the Nazi dictator, has cultivated a similar moustache and forelock. They come and stay with Hubert's family and William, convinced that Orford *is* Hitler, contrives to shut him in the Old Barn; he has decided that Robert (conveniently home on leave) must capture him from the hated Lanes and hand him over to 'the Government': 'He meant Robert to be a hero, therefore Robert must be a hero. It would have been easier to reconcile oneself to the old unheroic Robert had it not been for Hubert's cousin with his glorious prize . . .' His brother, comfortably installed in a deck-chair in the garden and immersed in a book, is reluctant to believe William's story of a German parachutist being imprisoned in the barn but, eventually, he is persuaded to investigate. When he opens the barn door, Lt. Orford attacks him ferociously, and Robert gives as good (or

bad) as he gets – but they soon abandon their fight, explain matters to their mutual satisfaction and become friends. (By this time Orford has become 'bored to death with Hubert's cousin and the Lanes'.) Realizing that he has had his leg pulled by Hubert, William – in common with thousands of his fellow-countrymen – begins to realize that 'It's a rotten war.'

He does, in fact, have the satisfaction of being concerned with the capture of at least three Nazi spies (though during the course of the war he wrongly suspects many more than that number of harmless citizens of being German agents). In *William and the Brains Trust* he indirectly helps Finch (a member of British Intelligence disguised as a tramp) to round up two spies – the supposed Austrian refugee 'Miss Smith' (Fräulein Schmitt, who has been working at the vicarage) and her colleague, who is an unnamed man 'with a white moustache and a limp'. In *William and the Evacuees*, without meaning to do so, he alerts Wing-Commander Glover from

WILLIAM'S MOUTH DROPPED OPEN. HIS EYES GOGGLED. FOR AT A SIDE DOOR APPEARED A FIGURE LONG FAMILIAR TO HIM.

Marleigh Aerodrome (who is 'nuts on Ethel' and therefore in William's orbit) to the strange activities of Mr Redding, a visitor to the village whom William describes as 'the Bird Man'. He has found curious drawings in his cottage, which Redding says are of a blackbird's legs and a sparrow's stomach. William believes him, but they are actually sketches of the insides of parts of British planes – which Glover spots immediately when one falls out of Ethel's handbag (where William has put it as a practical joke). William naturally claims sole responsibility for the apprehension of this German spy.

It is, however, his less dramatic attempts to 'do his bit' for the war effort that strike echoes of real-life activities. The books already mentioned, together with *William Does His Bit*, *Just William's Luck* and *William the Bold*, provide indelible vignettes of William shoving a saucepan on his head as an improvised steel helmet and pressing a tin tray into action as a shield when trying to tackle a suspected unexploded bomb (see picture page 67), supplementing the nation's food supply by participating in organized fruit-picking, tangling with 'spiv' and 'wide-boy' black-marketeers, and being enthralled at the idea of tank-traps, shooting down enemy planes, helping to buy Spitfires, or inventing new explosives ('he had experimented with charcoal, sulphur and saltpetre in the greenhouse . . . but the only results had been a wrecked greenhouse, several minor injuries and the docking of his pocket-money for months to come').

During its early stages there are times when the Outlaws consider the war a nuisance rather than a stimulus. In *William and the Evacuees* they bemoan the fact that it has curtailed their activities: 'Farmers, laying out more land for vegetable growing, were impatient of trespassers', and uncaring adults were even more dismissive than usual of their offspring's demands upon their time and energies: 'I can't be bothered with you . . . There's a war on' was a common response. Two years later, in *William Carries On*, William reflects that the advantages and disadvantages of the war more or less cancel each other out. By now gamekeepers have been called up so he can trespass 'in woods and fields with comparative impunity'. Also, discipline has been relaxed at school, because of the 'gradual infiltration of women teachers', and at home because his father is having to work longer hours at the office while his mother is more pre-occupied than usual, having to manage without a cook. However, on the negative side sweets are scarce and cream buns 'unprocurable', there are no parties, summer holidays are out of the question 'because of something called the Income Tax, and for the same reason pocket money, inadequate at the best of times, had faded almost to vanishing point'. The Outlaws, with their customary resilience, endeavour to make the best of things, for example, using the Botts' luxuriously appointed underground air-raid shelter as a place in which to play at submarines, or getting the better of pompous, over-zealous A.R.P. wardens or fire-fighters.

Richmal Crompton had volunteered for the Auxiliary Fire Service early in the war, and she zestfully avenged herself on a bossy senior officer by letting William debunk his prototype in *William Does His Bit*. Putting out fires, of course, was something that the civilian population expected to have to do. Families were issued with stirrup pumps, and sandbags and buckets were always at the ready to cope with incendiary bombs during air-raids. However when an A.F.S. 'area' is established at Hadley garage the Outlaws are truly thrilled. As well as trailers, pumps 'and a heterogeneous collection of cars' there are 'miles of hose-pipe and a glorious spate of water', with 'God-like beings in long rubber boots reaching almost to their waists' wading about the wet garage floor, polishing the trailers and occasionally doing physical jerks. And on triumphant occasions they set out with their cars and trailers to nearby ponds, where they demonstrate their skills by unwinding the hoses and sending 'breathtaking' sprays of water in every direction. It is small wonder that

"GET OUT OF THIS AT ONCE!" THUNDERED THE SECTION OFFICER. "HOW DARE YOU COME IN HERE! DON'T YOU KNOW THAT YOU'RE TRESPASSING?"

the Outlaws, who – as usual – are whole-hearted in embracing a new activity, cannot stay away. They spend every possible waking moment at Hadley garage and have the satisfaction of 'helping' because most of the firemen are friendly: 'One of them let William hold a hose-pipe.'

The Outlaws decide to 'join 'em prop'ly', so William rummages ruthlessly through Ethel's work-box to find some red silk thread with which they laboriously sew the letters 'A.F.S.' on to their coats. The resulting 'spidery hieroglyphics' look more like 'laundry marks gone mad' than a badge of Government service, but William thinks they pass muster. He marches Ginger, Henry and Douglas through the main street of Hadley and into the garage and, when the men go on parade, the Outlaws take their places at the end of the line and stand smartly to attention. So far, so

satisfying. But a rude shock awaits them in the shape of Section Officer Perkins, 'a youthful platinum blond, with an exaggerated idea of his own importance'. Suspecting that the participation of the Outlaws makes him look ridiculous, he not only tells them furiously that they are trespassing and bans them from the garage, but even forbids them to stand outside and watch the firemen's exciting procedures.

William and his friends have the consolation of starting their own branch of the fire service (absolutely unofficial, of course) on some waste-land near by, but without proper equipment or contact with the professionals this activity soon begins to pall, and the odious Section Officer Perkins makes matters worse by spying on and sneering at them. Things come to a head when William, in good faith, gets Perkins's men called out to what he thinks is a real fire but is actually a false alarm. They are then told by their enemy that he will go and see their fathers that evening and demand that they receive dire punishment. On the basis that they might as well be hanged for a sheep as a lamb, William decides to rig up a booby-trap at Perkins's home. He explains his plan to his henchmen; they will set up a bucket of water to fall on the Section Officer when he opens the door. William chuckles in anticipation: 'As usual, he saw the scheme in its finished perfection, magnificently ignoring the intervening details.'

When they get to Perkins's home they find it is on fire, but using buckets of water and a great deal of determination they extinguish the flames. By the time the Captain of the regular Fire Brigade (somewhat in rivalry with the A.F.S.) arrives, 'these plucky boys'. with their faces blackened beyond recognition receive him proudly. Perkins then comes on the scene and has to suffer a reprimand from the Captain who realizes that the fire has started because a burning cigarette has accidentally been left by Perkins in the house. The Outlaws are jubilant at his discomfiture and at the Captain's appreciation of their efforts. There is a double irony in this episode: William and his friends have saved Perkins's house from major fire damage – but they went there to avenge themselves on him – while he – the great fire-fighter – was inadvertently responsible for starting the blaze.

One of the most significant and disruptive social changes of the war was the wholesale evacuation of children from towns and cities to so-called safe areas, and William becomes involved with evacuees in several of the books. In *William and the Evacuees* the dreaded Arabella Simpkin with a band of village children declares that, as evacuees get 'all the fun', William should arrange to have the local children evacuated. He argues reasonably that there is little chance of their village being bombed, but Arabella caustically replies that, 'It's nothing' to do with bombs . . . why don't you listen? It's to do with parties and clothes an' tins of sweets an' things . . .' She is, of course, commenting on the goodies provided by the local ladies for evacuees who have come to them from the danger areas. William, thus appealed to, dare not admit that the task of transferring most of the village children into new homes elsewhere is beyond him, but he is soon hit by the enormity of his task. However, 'then he consoled himself by the reflection that the government had evacuated whole towns in a few hours without a hitch. William considered himself as good as the government any day . . .' He *does* get them all into a new home but it is not far away, and they are soon restored to the bosoms of their families.

In another story the enmity between some young evacuees and the local children is tellingly conveyed. Violet Elizabeth has a party which offers ices and cakes in pre-war proportions. Her guests are exhorted to save some of these for the deprived evacuees who have come to live in the village but, instead, they fall on the feast with furious intensity, and mop up the last crumb. This is because the local children feel that they have suffered much at the hands of 'the tough young guys from London' and are determined that their tormentors will not share their gastronomic treat.

Another important alteration on the Home Front scene is the defection of cooks, housemaids, gardeners and so on into war work on the land, in munitions factories or 'on the buses'. The Browns' somewhat elastic household visibly shrinks during the 1940s and like so many real-life ones is never restored to its pre-war glories. In *William Does His Bit* we are told that cook has gone to join the forces and that Emma, the housemaid, is the sole surviving domestic servant. However, we know that Cook still reigns over the kitchen in the early part of the book because one of the war economies then mentioned is that she now has to mix butter and margarine together. Other shortages detailed are Mrs Brown's having to make a cake with egg substitute and Ethel's need to wear her silk stockings even when there is a darn in the front where it shows: 'I'd rather have *died* than be seen with a darn there before the war.' Robert has to give

"COOK," SAID WILLIAM, "HOW DO PEOPLE GET TO BE WAR PROFITEERS?"
"YOU LEAVE THEM SULTANAS ALONE, MASTER WILLIAM," SHE SAID STERNLY.

up his motor-bike. Mr Brown yearns vainly for Stilton cheese while Mrs Brown feels that her three-year-old fur coat is falling apart but that it cannot be replaced. William is worried about the increased price – and shorter sucking time – of wartime Monster Humbugs. His idea of solving the problem of shortages is to suggest the economy of his not going to school any more, which will save his father from having to pay the fees. He also offers to give up clothes 'an' paint myself same as the Anshunt Britons'.

'"D'you know," said William thoughtfully at breakfast [in *William Carries On*] "I don't seem to remember the time there wasn't a war."' His mother tells him not to be ridiculous as the war has only lasted for two years and he is eleven – but, with a sigh, she agrees: 'I know what you mean.'

In the books, as in fact, the mood shifts from patriotic endeavour to cussed resentment of officialdom and restrictions, and to some dabbling in the black market. The Botts, for example, use their money to insulate themselves against at least some of the wartime shortages. They manage to acquire supplies of fancy cakes and chocolate biscuits while the Outlaws have to lament the loss of bull's-eyes and bars of milk chocolate, as well as pistol caps.

For Mrs Bott the main disadvantages of the war are the rudeness of shopkeepers and the disappearance of smoked salmon and decent bacon. In fact Botty, who has abandoned the making of his celebrated sauce for the duration, is doing very well 'in the way of war contracts'. In *William Does His Bit* she is approached by the Dig for Victory Committee, headed by General Moult, to allow the park of the Hall to be used for allotments. Not surprisingly Mrs Bott doesn't take kindly to this suggestion; 'Right up to our winders that park comes, remember. What about me an' Botty with a lot of common men trampin' about just outside the 'ouse and starin' in at us when we're 'aving our meals?' She goes on and on, resisting both persuasion (the suggestion that a fence or hedge will keep the enthusiastic vegetable-growers well out of sight of the house) and coercion (an implication from Mr Brown, a member of the committee, that 'official pressure' could be brought to bear): 'Mrs Bott's small eyes gleamed with rage. "You try what you calls hofficial pressure on me, Mr John Brown, an' I cancels hevery single subscription I gives to this 'ere bloomin' village!"' The committee know that they must bow to this because without her bountiful contributions most of the local organizations could hardly be carried on.

General Moult makes a last attempt to intimidate her by assuming the ferocious expression which had once caused both recruits and young officers to tremble but 'it glanced off Mrs Bott like a pin off a tank'. She simply tells him to stop trying on his 'harmy hairs and graces', reiterates extremely forcibly that no one will be doing any 'muckin' about' in her 'hornamental pleasure park' and orders the committee to 'git out'. She advances on them with flushed cheeks and her eyes alight for battle, and the six strong men on the Dig for Victory Committee, including General Moult, 'who in his youth had faced hordes of charging Zulus unperturbed', are ignominiously put to flight.

Needless to say William succeeds where grown men have failed. He and Ginger find that a large wooden 'Unexploded Bomb' notice has been temporarily abandoned by the side of a country lane awaiting removal later that day by the authorities (the bomb had been a false alarm anyway). They decide to borrow it for the 'war museum' show they are putting on that afternoon to raise money for the Spitfire fund but, after carrying it some distance and finding it rather heavy, they go off in search of help from Henry and Douglas and dump the notice *pro tem* just outside the gates of the Hall. Of course Mrs Bott returns from a shopping expedition while it is there, and, hysterically, thinking that a bomb has been dropped on her grounds as a sign that she should do more for the war effort, she hurries into the Browns' house nearby and signs the agreement (which William's father

"COME BACK!" MR. LEICESTER SHOUTED
HOARSELY. "COME *BACK!* YOU – YOU – YOU—"
WORDS FAILED HIM.

just happens to have handy) for making the park over to allotments. Mr Brown, urged by his wife to go and investigate the bomb situation on Mrs Bott's behalf, returns with the news that there *is* no notice (the Outlaws have, of course, now managed to lug it away). Far from suspecting dire and dirty doings, Mrs Bott is smugly intrigued because she thinks that the notice must have been a psychic vision on her part – and is thrilled to think that she has 'the gift' of second sight. There is a bonus in all this for William. While Mrs Bott stands outside the Hall, contemplating her good fortune that it is still intact and that she has access to 'vishuns', William slouches by, disconsolate because the Outlaws' war museum show has been a failure. Mrs Bott is moved to placate the mystic universal powers still further by handing William three pounds – which is even more than his hoped-for target of money to be raised by the show for the Spitfire Fund.

Of course the war eventually ground to its end in 1945, and the stories of the mid and late 40s show William involved

in the processes of reconstruction and rehabilitation that marked the beginning of peacetime. First, however, the Outlaws arrange a victory celebration. Henry suggests a 'vict'ry ball' but William dismisses that because it would mean involving girls and dancing, to both of which he is opposed. They settle on the idea of a Victory Pageant and, despite William's reservations about the opposite sex, Joan (at the Outlaws' request) and Violet Elizabeth (without invitation) are at first included. The plan is that Joan will represent Britannia (though Violet Elizabeth really wants to be this as her mother has a nice Britannia 'fanthy dreth cothtume'), the male Outlaws and some of their allies will take the roles of British soldiers, etc, and hopefully the Hubert Laneites might be persuaded to be German prisoners. Violet Elizabeth is grudgingly given the consolation prize of portraying Germany, but declines because William will not let her wear her dress with a skirt of 'pink thilk petalth' for this but insists that she should wear sackcloth daubed with swastikas. She walks out –

and, to the Outlaws' consternation, when they approach Hubert about his gang playing the parts of German prisoners he complacently refuses, and adds that Violet Elizabeth is now organizing a rival pageant to theirs, to take place on the same day at the Hall, with teas for cast and audience arranged by Mrs Bott. The plan for the pageant seems to be a complete copy of William's – except, of course, that Hubert & Co. are to play the triumphant British heroes, and that they would like to assign the roles of the defeated Germans to the Outlaws.

William, Ginger, Henry and Douglas are not only shocked by Violet Elizabeth's perfidy; they find that they miss

"I'VE GOT A LOVELY THURPRITHE FOR YOU, WILLIAM,"
SAID VIOLET ELIZABETH.

her enlivening presence at rehearsals (and even begin to realize that Joan is submissive to the point of irritation). They doggedly persist with their rehearsals, minus the cantankerous Miss Bott and also any boys who are prepared to play the German parts. William has decided that the performance will take place in the grounds of Marleigh Manor because its owners, Sir Gerald and Lady Markham, will be away in Scotland and its gardener spends all day in his greenhouse doing football pools and is, anyway, too deaf to notice anything going on.

He and his motley-dressed cast assemble there (their improvised uniforms are more suggestive of Robin Hood, Red Indians and rather mothy Knights of the Round Table than of the British army) to find lots of bored and listless children sitting in neat rows on the lawn. This is not quite the audience that was expected, but William plunges into the victory pageant.

Joan, as Britannia, has just made her opening rhyming address (both she and William are rather proud of her ability to write 'po'try') when the proceedings are interrupted by Violet Elizabeth, clad triumphantly in pink silk as Germany, leading the marching figures of the Hubert Laneities. "'I wath only teathing you, William,' she said. 'I've got a lovely thurprithe for you.'" She has delivered the Laneites into the hands of the Outlaws like lambs to the slaughter, by persuading them that it would be easy to break up William's pageant and force him and his followers to play the hated parts of the German prisoners. Of course, William & Co. instead inflict these roles on Hubert and his gang. Violet Elizabeth has indeed brought off a coup. William's triumph is complete when Lady Markham appears, overcome with gratitude. This is the afternoon when she has arranged an entertainment for slum children (the originally bored and listless audience) at the manor but unfortunately the conjuror and Punch and Judy man whom she had engaged have both cried off at the last moment because of indisposition. No other suitable professional entertainers could be obtained at such short notice, so William's stepping into the breach (as she sees it) is heaven-sent. She regards the pageant – which ends in the usual free fight – as a rather delightful children's Battle of Flowers. The performers are, of course, invited to join the slum children in a tea which, even in wartime, manages to be lavish.

The story, as it appeared in *William the Bold*, omitted one or two important details which had been included in its original publication (in the magazine *Modern Woman* in May 1946). This explains how Violet Elizabeth had duped Hubert & Co. into donning garb appropriate to the Nazi leaders. Hubert (whom she introduces to the audience as 'ole Goering') had been told he was to play Churchill and should wear a row of medals, Bertie Franks (announced as 'the ole Fuehrer') has corked in a moustache on the assumption that he will be representing Mr Anthony Eden, while Claude Bellew (cast by her as 'ole Goebbleth the liar') thinks he is to be General Montgomery. Violet Elizabeth, not to be outdone by the poetic Joan, performs her part in rhyme, starting with:

'I am ole Germany,
Beat in the war,
A goothe that won't go goothe-thtepping
Any more.'

(It is interesting to speculate on why her 'poetic' introductions of the characters, several verses in all, and the naming of Churchill, Eden, Monty, etc. were omitted from the story when it was published in *William the Bold*. This was in 1950, four years after its appearance in *Modern Woman*. Was it because the public's memory of the Nazi – and wartime British – leaders was considered to be too short? Or because by then the ironic

motif of Noel Coward's popular song 'Don't let's be beastly to the Germans' had become national policy?)

In *William and the Brains Trust* the Outlaws anticipate the concept of 'pupil power', which was not to achieve any degree of recognition until the late 1970s. Inspired by adult talk of social reconstruction after the publication of the Beveridge Report, William declares that, as this will only look after grown-ups, an Outlaws' Report is required to meet the needs of the younger generation. After a great deal of discussion the document is prepared, and William hatches an elaborate scheme to get it to London so that the government can make it an Act of Parliament. His plans go wildly awry; his report never gets to the Government but, in a happy mix-up that is typical of a William-engineered plot, the story ends with the Outlaws being promised a visit to a Christmas pantomime:

The Outlaws' drooping spirits soared. 'Hurrah!'

They have, of course, realized 'that a pantomime in the hand is worth a dozen Acts of Parliament in the bush . . .'

Their Report is given here in full:

Outlaws Report
Habby. Ass. Corpuss.
Magner Carter.

1. As much hollidays as term
2. No afternoon school.
3. Sixpence a week pocket munny and not to be took off.
4. No Latin no French no Arithmetick.
5. As much ice creem and banarnas and creem buns as we like free.
6. No punnishments and stay up as late as we like.

WILLIAM
AND THE
MOON ROCKET

RICHMAL CROMPTON

The 1950s – William the Expansive

When the 1950s began there was both a looking back to the bleak days of war and a looking forward to a hoped-for period of economic rehabilitation, social security and new opportunities for all. At the beginning of the decade food and clothes were still rationed and many ordinary, as well as luxury, goods remained in short supply. But the mood was one of recovery and the ending of austerity, as well as of national pride and relief at having survived the war. It was evident that the war had permanently changed certain social patterns: many wives and mothers as well as single girls who had worked in industry or the services were determined to stay in regular jobs rather than to be at home. Except for the most affluent of families, domestic service had become virtually unobtainable. The democratization process continued abroad as well as at home, and the Empire was breaking up to become the more participatory Commonwealth. The widely celebrated 1951 Festival of Britain projected the new atmosphere of expansion through scientific discovery and the demolition of social and national barriers.

William, of course, reflected something of all this in his aspirations and achievements during the 50s, and his village – though still in many ways remarkably impervious to change and challenge – was also to be affected by the Welfare State, the National Health Service and ideals of greater democracy. Just like many people of the time in real life, William had one foot firmly planted in the past (still, for instance, liking tramps and thrilling to the idea of becoming one) and the other in the future (planning with Ginger to get to the moon many years before technology was sufficiently advanced to allow lunar exploration).

William's popularity had reached a peak during the late 1940s, with the radio programmes giving him fresh and wider worlds to conquer. The 50s saw the production of various 'spin-offs' from the books but, though William was becoming an ever more deeply estab-lished household word and household face, only four William books were pub-lished during the decade: *William and the Tramp* (1952), *William and the Moon Rocket* (1954), *William and the Space Animal* (1956) and *William's Television Show* (1958). (*William – the Bold* had appeared in 1950 but it reprinted 1940s stories, several of which still had a war-time flavour.) One reason why there were fewer books than in earlier decades might have been the acute paper short-ages of the early 50s, which frustrated publishers of both books and magazines. Another was possibly that, after Sep-tember 1954, the stories no longer appeared in magazines (and to regular deadlines) before being collected into books. After the *Happy Mag* ended in 1940, the stories had appeared fairly regularly in *Modern Woman* until the middle of the decade, then in *Homes & Gardens* and *Home Notes*, but the one-story-every-month pattern that had held

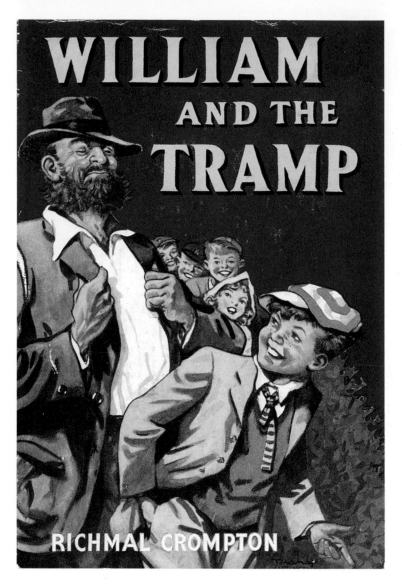

WILLIAM AND THE TRAMP

RICHMAL CROMPTON

good for so long in the *Happy Mag* was not perpetuated. It is also possible that Richmal, who was sixty years old at the beginning of the 1950s, wanted to take things somewhat easier. However, she was certainly not running out of ideas for the books, which were as inventive and zestful as in previous decades.

It seems that, in spite of being hoodwinked by tramps who have cropped up earlier in his life, William remains perpetually trusting of and fascinated by these colourful vagabonds. In the eponymous opening story of *William and the Tramp*, the Outlaws' reforming

zeal is stimulated by Henry's mother's interest in a campaign for 'gettin' holiday homes for poor ole people what have never had a holiday'. Just as they and Violet Elizabeth are discussing this they encounter a bearded and tousled tramp sitting by the side of a ditch and tucking into a simple meal of bread and cheese. Having by now decided that there is room in the vastness of the Botts' home for some poorer members of the community to have a holiday, William decides to install the tramp there, promising rich food as well as warm shelter. The tramp, who gives his name somewhat improbably as Marmaduke Mehitavel, gets both, because, cleaned up and provided by Violet Elizabeth with one of her father's suits, he is mistaken by Mrs Bott for Mr Bumbleby, who is due to arrive at the Hall that day to address the Literary Society about conditions in modern South Africa.

Violet Elizabeth has suffered some apprehension that her mother may not like Marmaduke – 'I think thee'th going to think he'th common' – but he enters so fully into the spirit of the affair that Mrs Bott is charmed and honoured by his presence in her gracious home. The meeting is held in her new 'garden room', of which she is immensely proud, but just as Mr Marmaduke Mehitavel takes his seat and prepares to address the audience, the genuine lecturer arrives and has to be kept out of the way by the Outlaws. Mr Bumbleby, a fellow of the Royal Geographical Society and a much travelled author, joins the considerable ranks of those unfortunate speakers who have come to meetings in William's village and been waylaid and diverted before finding their promised audience. Ginger, Douglas and Violet Elizabeth guide him through the unlit garden and take advantage of his disorientation to lock him in the coal-shed. Later, when he manages to break out of this, he is not home and dry because in his grimy, gasping and belligerent state he is mistaken for the tramp whose presence around the village has been noted by the vicar earlier in the day. Mr Bumbleby is nearly arrested but is saved by the fact that the genuine tramp uses the diversion caused by the lecturer's arrival to take himself – and Mrs Bott's famed diamond brooch – swiftly off the scene.

Some special and party foodstuffs were still in short supply in the early 50s, and the promise of being invited to a party which will offer four different kinds of ices as well as jelly and strawberries is enough to tempt several of William's school-mates into entering a historical essay competition. As well as an invitation to this end-of-term party at Rose Mount School for Girls, its Headmistress, Miss Priscilla Golightly, is offering a prize for the best essay, which is to be judged by her nephew Justinian, who has just been appointed Professor of History at 'one of the older universities'. William has no interest in the prize, though he dashes off an essay just to prove to himself and the Outlaws – who find it impressive – that he is as good as the next boy. (It should be noted that there is no improvement in his spelling over the decades.)

His essay is short if not sweet:

> Bony prince charly
> He came bekause they playd skotsh chunes on bag peips he dansed with ladies and fort a battel and fel into a bogg and then there wasent ennything elce to do so he went hoam in a botc.

He soon has the opportunity of showing it to the Professor (when both of them are hiding for different reasons from the redoubtable Priscilla Golightly), who says that he likes it much better than the essay which will eventually get the prize. William is flattered, but admits that Douglas thought some of the spelling wasn't right: '"It's the spelling I like best of all," said Professor Golightly.' William's conversation with him, while they are concealed behind packing cases in a cupboard under Miss Golightly's stairs and eating her entire store of sultanas, symbolizes the increasingly democratic feeling between adults and children, and teachers and pupils, during the 1950s. When the coast is clear enough for them to leave the store cupboard, William introduces the illustrious Professor to

WILLIAM WAS PRECIPITATED ON TO THE HEAD OF THE UNFORTUNATE MR. BUMBLEBY.

the delights of Monster Humbugs and the Wall of Death at Hadley Fair.

It is because of Joan that William visits Miss Golightly's rooms. She is now a pupil at Rose Mount School and begs William to help her over 'a matter of life and death', which turns out to be the Headmistress's confiscation of a powder compact which Joan has bought for her mother's birthday present. William is rather more reluctant than in the past to rush to Joan's aid: he *does* – he thinks – retrieve the compact, but it turns out to be the wrong one, and he doesn't even bother

"OH, WILLIAM, I'M SO MISERABLE," CRIED JOAN,
"AND I WANT YOU TO HELP ME."

to go to Joan's party afterwards because the Wall of Death and Professor Golightly's company prove to be a more attractive option. 'Suddenly . . . William found that he didn't care. He didn't even want to reinstate himself in Joan's eyes . . . The demands of womankind in general and Joan in particular were incessant and exacting.' This surely marks the end of an era; for decades Joan has been William's romantic inspiration, even though their relationship was of a spasmodic nature because of her family's periods of removal from the village. She is the only girl ever to have been honoured by full membership of the Outlaws – but all that now seems to be forgotten. Is William at last beginning to grow up a little? At any rate he has apparently freed himself from his long-term emotional dependence on Joan.

It is perhaps significant that his grown-up idols still maintain their hold

on his imagination and loyalty. Archie returns to his cottage from abroad, overflowing with admiration for Ethel and friendship towards William and the Outlaws. Their protectiveness of him is shown when he arranges to have a party, mainly because he hopes that the fair Ethel will come, and William diverts a group of art buyers to go to it (because he realizes that he has forgotten to post the invitations which Archie has earlier entrusted to him). William can't bear the thought of Archie being disappointed and is determined that he shall have a party. The art buyers purchase some of his pictures too – though they return them when they realize that Archie's is not the art sale at Marleigh which they expected to attend. However, Archie is not too disappointed by this because he sees Ethel returning with friends from the tennis club, and calls them in to join the party. In *William and the Moon Rocket* William and Ginger again feel obliged to look after Archie when they suspect (wrongly of course) that he is a criminal who must leave the country immediately if he is to avoid arrest. They persuade him to get into a van with his current 'masterpiece', a reclining figure which he plans to enter in the forthcoming Hadley art exhibition. Even to the loyal William this massive, crudely hewn statue doesn't suggest, actually or symbolically, a human figure – but it has the astoundingly positive effect of arousing Ethel's appreciation. A mix-up of instructions causes the van-driver to deliver Archie to the Browns' house, where Ethel and the Amateur Dramatic Society are having a party. (Archie thinks that he and his stone figure are on their way to the Hadley art gallery: the Outlaws think he is on his way to Portsmouth, a boat and freedom from the reach of the law.) The Thespians need a very special seat for the play which they are rehearsing and have been let down by someone who promised a suitable one; Archie's reclining figure is received with enthusiasm: 'Isn't it lovely! . . . It's got just that touch of magic and mystery.' 'Archie, you're wonderful!' They all think, of course, that he has made them an

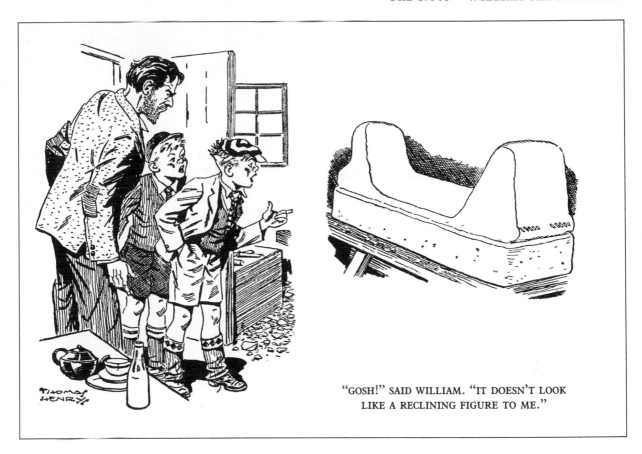

"GOSH!" SAID WILLIAM. "IT DOESN'T LOOK
LIKE A RECLINING FIGURE TO ME."

absolutely appropriate seat for their play
and Archie, basking in Ethel's grateful
smiles, wisely decides not to put his
work of art into the Hadley Exhibition.

Ethel and Robert are still involved in
intense on and off romances, although
we are told that Ethel is slimming now,
and presumably keeping a watchful eye
on her charms to ensure that these are in
no danger of fading. Between more
exciting affairs she falls back on Archie
and, to a lesser extent now, on Jimmie
Moore, with whom she was supposed
during the 40s to have been in love. In
William and the Space Animal he drops
in for the evening but now seems more
like a friend than a lover, and the last
mention of him in the saga comes in
William's Television Show: it seems that
their romance has been nipped in the
bud. Richmal surely realized that
Ethel's quintessential role in William's
world was that of the ever nubile but
always not-quite-ready-to-settle-down

heroine. Until the 1950s it was sufficient
to have Mrs Brown established as the
only permanently domesticated female
of the family, patiently 'yes-dear'-ing as
she made and mended the socks of her
menfolk. However, in *William's Television Show* she rather surprisingly
begins to wonder if she has wasted her
life. (She has been used as a model by a
cosmetics demonstrator, and is looking
more elegant and assured than usual.)
She yearns to go to certain places and to
participate in specific events that have
not previously attracted her – Ascot, a
Buckingham Palace garden party and
the Olympic Games, for instance. William and the Outlaws decide to indulge
her with far more excitement by staging
their own Olympic Games for her to see
and, while they are practising throwing
the hammer (in someone else's garden)
they inadvertently stun a burglar.
The occupant, Mr Tertullian Selwyn,
gratefully offers William almost any

WILLIAM'S TELEVISION SHOW

RICHMAL CROMPTON

reward he can think of and, wanting to give his mother the special present of 'a thoughtful act' for her birthday, William arranges that Mr Selwyn will pay for remedying the dry rot in the village hall platform – something that will give Mrs Brown great satisfaction and, presumably, assuage the restlessness she has been experiencing.

The 1950s have seen remarkable changes in William's father. His attitude towards his younger son seems more tolerant and democratic: William regularly addresses him as 'Dad' rather than father – and so does Robert – and he seems much more approachable. Astoundingly, in *William and the Moon Rocket*, he takes William and Ginger to the fair (although he is led there somewhat unsuspectingly), treats them to turns on many thrilling things, and walks home with them carrying a coconut under each arm. Then, in another episode in the same book, he takes them to see the Wonder Cossack show.

Of all William's relatives during the 1950s it is Robert who behaves least satisfactorily when – as so often – he is temporarily but almost totally under the influence of one or another pretty but petulant girl. In *William and the Tramp* he is under the spell of Dolores Forrester, who has a cissy six-year-old brother, Peregrin. William would normally ignore this character or treat him with contempt, but he realizes that, in order to curry favour with his inamorata, Robert is passing to the despised Peregrin several perquisites which should rightly come William's way. Miss Milton meanwhile is arranging a children's entertainment, based on nursery-rhyme characters wearing Kate Greenaway costumes, to celebrate the 1951 Festival of Britain. She gives the prettiest and most docile juveniles (including, of course, Peregrin) speaking or solo-singing parts, and decides that all the other and more awkward, lumpy and charmless children will simply walk or skip about the stage in a grand finale representing 'Boys and Girls Come Out to Play' (William naturally is cast as one of these but bitterly resents having to be involved at all in such a soppy business). Robert's

THE HAMMER FLEW THROUGH THE AIR, OVER THE HEDGE INTO THE GARDEN OF BRENT HOUSE.

graciousness towards Peregrin continues, despite William's very vocal protests, and things come to a head when he offers to give him his collection of birds' eggs. Robert has cherished this for years, and knows in his heart that he is committing fearful perfidy against William in giving the collection – for which his brother has unusual reverence – to Peregrin, but he has succumbed weakly to 'sweetly wistful' but strong hints from Dolores that favours from her might follow. However, for once Mrs Brown

MR. BROWN, WILLIAM AND GINGER AFTER A PROFITABLE HOUR AT THE FAIR.

takes a strong line, and so does his father. They feel that William should not be bypassed. Dolores cunningly suggests that Robert should be allowed to present the collection as a prize to the child who is judged by Sir Ross Lewes – a local retired actor – the best performer in Miss Milton's entertainment. As she points out to Robert, 'Peregrin's sure to get it. Everyone says that his Little Tom Tucker scene is too sweet for words.'

The great day of the Festival of Britain performance arrives. William and most of the cast of the 'Boys and Girls Come Out to Play' scene decide to

turn up at the last minute. First they will hold a meeting of the Pets Club, which William has recently started, in the Old Barn. They are wearing their Greenaway garb, which after some good-natured scuffles with both human and animal members of the club gets slightly the worse for wear. William's costume in particular gets so badly torn that it is no longer decent. Instead he puts on the only 'clothes' that are readily available – a frayed and moth-eaten chenille curtain. When the moment comes for the final scene of the nursery-rhyme entertainment he leads 'a crowd of tatterdemalion children and barking dogs' across the stage: there are rats and cats too, for good measure. Sir Ross, who has until then been intensely bored by the whole proceedings, roars with delight and presents the birds'-egg collection prize to William: 'He was excellent . . . He seemed to embody the whole carefree spirit of vagabondage. A most spirited performance.'

During the 50s Mrs Brown is not only managing with far less domestic help but has a closer and more friendly relationship with her 'daily', Mrs Peters, than ever she had in the days when she could employ housemaids. Almost certainly she knows that the only way to keep 'helps' now is to be nice to them and treat then democratically. In *William and the Moon Rocket* there is a vignette of Mrs Brown and Mrs Peters washing up together and chatting about the latter's social life rather more like friends than mistress and servant. It seems that the Browns still have some help from a part-time and unnamed gardener, although Mr Brown is now expected to do quite a lot of the outdoor work himself.

Robert, who has ditched Dolores and is now courting Roxana Mayfield (of whom William, unusually, approves), no longer struggles to run a car but has gone back to a motor-bike. There has been a strange reversion for William too; the hated dancing classes which he was allowed to abandon back in the thirties have now been re-instituted, though he is surprisingly unprotesting about this 'mental torcher'. In *William and the*

THE CROWD OF TATTERDEMALION CHILDREN AND BARKING DOGS RUSHED ACROSS THE STAGE.

Space Animal it seems that Ethel has moved somewhat with the times. In the earlier books, apart from her spells of war work, she never seemed to be gainfully employed. However, William now makes the startling statement that his sister is 'sick of her job', although we do not learn the nature of this. William and the Outlaws try to find her a new one, but their plans for this are as cock-eyed as their efforts in the 20s (see page 19) to get her a husband. Their image of her is indicated by the jobs which they consider appropriate: these are working as a 'plain cook' (they decide she can't do this as she's too pretty), as a companion-help, as a dog-sitter, a film-star or a spy.

William still feels moved to campaign for young people's rights when he hears about all the benefits which seem to come to members of the village's Over Sixty Club: he starts an Over Ten Club, hoping to muscle in on their perks, but without significant success. Signs of the times are that when he suspects Mr Kellyngs, the current occupant of Honeysuckle Cottage, of spying, he is convinced that he is selling atomic secrets to the Russians. (He is actually a harmless writer-cum-naturalist.) William therefore disguises himself in Ethel's jockey cap, Robert's golfing blouse and a straggling false moustache as Stalin, and melodramatically demands the atom bomb secrets: 'I'll send thee a postal order from Russia when I get there. Hist! Not a word! Give me the papers and begone!' The blameless author starts to simmer with fury but suddenly changes moods when he spots a spider, acquired by the Outlaws from the grocer's boy who discovered it in a crate of bananas. This is the tarantula that he has lusted after for years. Douglas resignedly expresses relief that the suspected spy 'didn't wade in our blood, anyway'.

In *William and the Moon Rocket* the eponymous equipment is not real but designed for funfairs and circuses. Nevertheless William's interest in lunar travel is genuine: 'We've got to be first on the moon,' he declares to Ginger, deploring the fact that he has already been pre-empted by other intrepid

"DID YOU ENJOY THE OVER-SIXTY CLUB MEETING YESTERDAY, MRS. PETERS?" ASKED MRS. BROWN.

"IT'S THE ONLY ONE IN ENGLAND AN' IT'S JOLLY VALU'BLE," SAID WILLIAM.

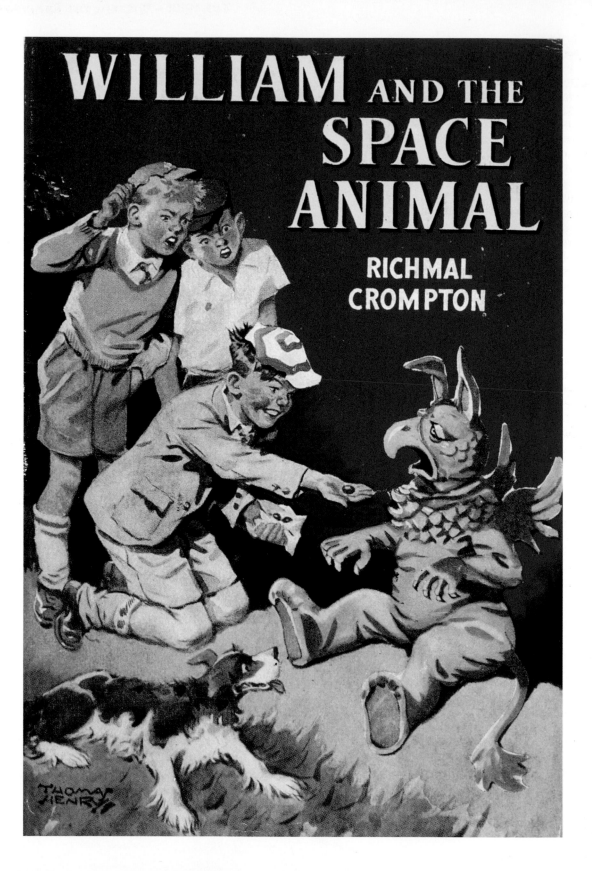

WILLIAM AND THE SPACE ANIMAL

RICHMAL CROMPTON

heroes from being the first to climb Everest or to reach the North Pole. Rather surprisingly his interest in Spacemen is limited: he thinks they look 'jolly dull . . . all covered up like tanks or washing-machines . . . It's a Space animal I want to see.' It seems that his wish is granted when in *William and the Space Animal* he is suddenly confronted by an unfamiliar creature with a long tail and a scaly skin, but it is only a small boy, Billy Clayton, who is garbed as a gryphon for a fancy-dress party and whose headpiece has become so firmly stuck that it seems to muffle not only his voice but also his intelligence.

One extremely popular and undoubtedly real factor of 1950s life that crops up in the stories is television. It was taken into many homes in 1953 when families wanted to watch the coronation of Queen Elizabeth II on the small screen and it is first mentioned in William's saga when he and Ginger, coerced into baby-sitting, are told that the television is out of order (in *William and the Space Animal*). In the next book, *William and the Television Show*, the Outlaws accurately interpret the addictiveness of the goggle-box. William talks of producing a play in the Old Barn but Douglas says gloomily that no one will come to watch it: 'They all want television plays now. They don't want real ones.' William, ever optimistic, is undeterred. He will put on a television show by the simple expedient of tearing a large hole in a sheet, which will reveal to the audience only the faces of the actors. His 'reel live tellyvishun sho not just pitchers' is a success which even the deeply cynical Arabella Simpkin cannot manage to disrupt – such is the power and reflected glory of this compelling medium.

William is at his most exuberant in *William and the Moon Rocket* when he and the Outlaws decide, as Henry puts it, that they 'ought to be doin' somethin' about bein' New Elizabethans' to mark the occasion of Queen Elizabeth II's coronation. They decide to emulate Sir Francis Drake and other great sea-dogs from the time of Elizabeth I and similarly to 'take treasures off

WILLIAM AND GINGER, FESTOONED WITH RED, WHITE AND BLUE, TRUNDLED THE BARROW, WHILE HENRY AND DOUGLAS MARCHED IN FRONT CARRYING FLAGS.

foreigners' and give them to England. There seems, however, to be a dearth of foreigners in the village just then, so they decide instead to discover a new country, by digging. They uncover a valuable collection of silver which belongs to Mr Kirkham, who is the current mayor. He is appropriately public-spirited, and having lived happily enough for years without the family silver decides that he will sell it and consult with the Outlaws about how the proceeds can best be spent to help the country. They are proud of his reassurance that they have 'found foreign treasure an' given it to the country . . . Same as Drake' and that they truly are 'New Elizabethans'. The episode ends with the Outlaws playing a game of darts with the mayor, during the course of which Ginger notices that Hubert Lane, who has been away from home, has now returned. With both old and new Elizabethan images ringing in his brain William grins, pauses in his dart-throwing and says, 'There's time to finish the game an' beat the Laneites, too.'

The success of radio and television presentations of the stories in the 1950s widened the audience for William and stimulated a variety of merchandise from sheet music to games and jigsaw puzzles

Like a flash William vanished out of the door.

William took a last look at his home.

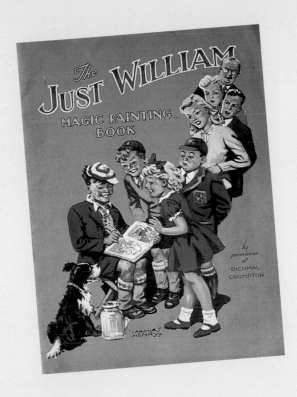

The 1960s – William the Campaigner

The 1960s were expansive years for people in Britain; the austerities and restrictions of wartime had, at last, been truly consigned to the past. This was the era of the Welfare State, of tolerance and permissiveness, flower power and pupil power; of the Beatles, the Rolling Stones and a proliferation of pop groups; these were the Swinging Sixties and they celebrated the culture of youth.

William, of course, was determined to play his full part in all this and to make vigorous use of the opportunities that came his way for greater involvement in local affairs, and participation in new and exciting causes.

In *William – the Explorer* (1960) the Outlaws are revelling in a deep fall of snow and an imaginary Arctic expedition when they see extraordinary footprints which suggest to them that the ''Bominable Snowman' is not far away. When they track the strange creature down they don't realize that he is really human, though he *is*, of course. He is Mr Jones, an elderly man who has a passion for going to fancy-dress parties; wearing a Mock Turtle outfit, he has lost his way in the snowstorm and can't get his headpiece off without assistance in order to explain things to the Outlaws. Eccentric but kindly, he lends William and his friends his skis and toboggan for rescuing him from his snow- and costume-bound plight.

By the 60s it had become fashionable for people of classes that some years earlier had been affluently leisured to take up paid work. Jobs were not then difficult to find, and William, aware of this, suddenly feels that he must work out a suitable career for Jumble, whose great talents are, he feels, going to waste. He has by now presumably given up completely on finding a job for Ethel (see page 79). The other Outlaws

"LOOK AT HIM," SAID WILLIAM PROUDLY. "I BET THERE WON'T BE ANOTHER P'LICE DOG IN THE WORLD TO TOUCH HIM."

do not entirely share William's touching belief in his pet's skills and prowess; they point out that when they've tried to train him as a St Bernard, a husky, a police dog, a regimental mascot or simply to chase a clockwork mouse he has proved far from adept. However, helping Jumble to make a success of his life becomes a crusade with William and, to his delight, he eventually finds something at which his doggy friend can excel. He has befriended a clown, through whose offices it is discovered that Jumble, a bit of a clown himself, works well as 'a circus dog'. Seeing Jumble perform with the clown at a children's party entertainment, 'William sat and watched, his heart full to bursting point.'

A further sign that William is influenced by contemporary social patterns occurs in *William – the Explorer* when he decides to take in a paying-guest, Miss Privet, in order to increase his always inadequate financial resources. At first Mr and Mrs Brown think that she is an aunt whom they are expecting from Australia – but misunderstandings are soon sorted out and the paying-guest experiment is extremely brief. It is interesting that Mr Brown, who now seems to have to care for his garden single-handed, feels that he'll be unable to cope with an extended visit from the Australian aunt, even without the paying-guest. Their house seems to shrink further with each decade.

A curious author who comes to the village, Cyprian Carruthers, has the leit motif of breaking the force of habit. William sits in on his conversation with Mr and Mrs Brown, in which he urges them to get out of their ruts. Learning that William's father always mows the lawn on Tuesdays, Cyprian exhorts him to claim his heritage 'as a free man' and leave the grass alone for once: '"It'd get a bit shaggy," said Mr Brown.' The earnest breaker of mental moulds then puts Mrs Brown in a spot by asking what she intends to do on the following day, and to those of us who have followed her fortunes over the decades her answer is predictable:

A ROAR OF APPLAUSE BROKE OUT.

'Oh . . . housework in the morning, I suppose . . . then the Women's Institute meeting in the afternoon and when I get home I shall set to work on the mending.'

Cyprian is so irritated by this that he knits his brows at her in a threatening fashion and demands to know if she always does her mending on Tuesdays. She placidly explains the logic of this: '. . . by Tuesday evening the washing's dried and ironed and aired, and it seems the best day to set to work on the mending.' Cyprian departs, Mr and Mrs Brown express to each other the fervent hope that he will never return – but they both admit that they are trapped in their ruts. William has been sufficiently impressed by their visitor's rhetoric to say 'Gosh!' and 'Crumbs!' (his favourite expletive) and to help break his parents' habits. It is, however, a losing battle. He laboriously carries his father's lawn-mower to a ditch just outside their front garden and hides it there, and he transfers his mother's work bag to a concealed place on a different shelf from its usual one. A few hours later, when he is expecting his mother and father to show their customary ingratitude for his 'help', Mr Brown most cordially thanks him for carrying the lawn-mower

"WHAT A MESS HE MADE OF IT!" SAID CELIA, TOSSING
HER HEAD. "MEN ARE INSUFFERABLE."

"THIS IS YOUR BIRTHDAY PARTY, GENERAL," SAID
MISS MILTON.

outside for the repair man to deal with a fault in it, and Mrs Brown is grateful to him for putting her bag in a dry place away from the small leak which has suddenly become evident just above its usual place. The lawn has been mown, and the socks have been darned, as always on a Tuesday.

William's Treasure Trove (1962) begins with his saying to Ginger 'Let's do somethin' we've never done before . . .' and Ginger replying 'We've done everything.' William *does* find a new activity, however; he rescues Aaron Myson, a seventy-eight-year-old pensioner, from the genteel boredom of incarceration in an old people's home – 'Won't let yer do nothin' but breathe an' 'ardly that,' Aaron grumbles. William rashly promises to find him a job and, by luck rather than judgement, gets General Moult to take him on as a gardener. The two elderly gents soon realize that they have much in common, as they are both retired military men and Boer War veterans. Aaron is soon promoted from jobbing gardener to become the General's resident secretary-companion-valet-housekeeper. His dependability and friendship mellow and humanize the peppery General from now until the end of the saga, when in *William – the Lawless* (1970) he and his many well-wishers celebrate his ninetieth birthday with a party and hearty singing of 'For He's a Jolly Good Fellow' and 'The Boys of the Old Brigade'. When Aaron asks the General how he is feeling he replies, with 'tears of emotion . . . in the dim, red-rimmed eyes', that he hasn't felt so happy 'since . . . the Relief of Mafeking'.

William is persuaded to take up 'detective journalism' at the insistence of Anthea Green, who thinks this will help her to start a juvenile branch of the literary society run by her sister Celia (who is Robert's current girl-friend). William responds to her request because 'there was a suggestion of wilfulness in her expression that brought the memory of Joan vividly to his mind'. (We are told that since Joan has moved he has 'preserved intact his armour of woman-hatred . . .' but this is not quite true.

Other females have cropped up in the interim whose attractions for him have helped to make the image of Joan fade to a mere shadow.) The process of detective journalism involves acting out the part of some imaginary person and interviewing a member of the public from this standpoint. It simply leads William into chaos, and Robert too, who is persuaded by Anthea's big sister to practise detective journalism at the front door of the house in which William is doing the same thing at the back door. The two sisters in the end huffily go away, feeling that William and Robert have failed them. Robert confides to William that he can't understand what he ever saw in Celia, and his brother replies 'Bossy . . . Whatever they start like they always end up bossy.' They are united in a brief bond of sympathy, but Robert suddenly feels bound to restore his elder-brother dignity: "You look as if you'd been dragged through a hedge backwards," he said severely. "Don't you ever brush your hair?"' This episode also involves Miss Milton, who, after reading a booklet called *How to Combat Old Age*, is following its advice of trying to feel younger by joining in a wider range of activities than usual – 'especially those organized by the younger set'. This doesn't work, of course, and she is soon reduced to hysterics.

Archie puts in another appearance in *William and the Witch* and is more inept, and more in love with Ethel, than ever. He helps run a hoop-la stall for a village fête and, as always, William looks after him. This book is the last to include Thomas Henry illustrations. He illustrated three of the stories before he died, and Henry Ford tackled the remaining two. Rubbing shoulders in this way, Henry Ford's pictures seem crude in comparison with Thomas Henry's – but they improved considerably as he became more experienced in depicting William's world. There is a fascinating episode in this book when William decides to become a psychiatrist (or rather a 'sekkitrist': he not only has difficulty in spelling this word but in remembering it, and exactly what he is supposed to be). He sets up as a psy-

chiatrist in the Old Barn after hearing that a famous member of that profession, Mr Summers, has left Harley Street to practise in Marleigh, and that all he does to cure 'mental troubles' is to let the patient talk and write down in a notebook what he or she says. William offers consultations at threepence each; his first patient is the morose Mr Peaslake, whose fiancée, Amanda, is threatening to break off their engagement. His second is Mr Summers himself, who feels badly in need of psychiatric treatment but is too proud to go to a more orthodox mind doctor. He tells William from the couch (in fact, the packing case) that he feels his life is totally devoid of colour. William and Ginger cure both patients by a single act; getting hold of some pots of red, blue, green and yellow paint, they decide to transform the inside of Mr Summers's home with this to give him the colour that he needs. However, they daub it all over Mr Peaslake's house by mistake. His fiancée is impressed when she sees it by what she thinks is Peaslake's innovative, 'pure *fauve*' décor: 'That unfinished look is too perfect . . . the very essence of primitive art.' Her reason for wanting to break off the engagement had been that he seemed too conventional and lacking 'in the vital spark', but she now sees him in a positive light and remains his fiancée. Mr Summers is called in by William to see this riot of colour and, when he realizes that it has been put into the wrong house, laughs long and heartily in a way that he has not done for years. He too is cured . . .

The same book provides an interesting vignette of Violet Elizabeth drunk with 'the lust of power that lives in every six-year-old breast'. She is to have her portrait painted and Mrs Bott allows her to choose whether Archie or Hubert Lane's relative, Tarquin, should be the artist. The Outlaws naturally press for Archie, while Hubert supports Tarquin's case. Violet Elizabeth lets Hubert bribe her with whatever sweets she wants and, knowing that William and his friends are having to 'woo' her, she rules the roost with relish: 'As William's squaw she bossed and bullied and nagged and tormented. There were times when the Outlaws' loyalty to Archie was strained almost to breaking point, but they held on doggedly.' And, as always, the precocious little Miss Bott comes down firmly on their – and Archie's – side at the end.

In *William and the Pop Singers* (1965), the Outlaws, as strolling players, meet a pop group called the Argonauts. The four young male performers punctuate their songs with 'Yeah! Yeah!' Yeah!' and are reminiscent of the Beatles, who were then in their heyday. Chris, the lead singer and composer, feels that he is wasting his life on trivialities but when William tells him about the play (written

by him and which his strolling players are going to act), with its space and lunar exploration theme, he rushes off and quickly composes a 'moon girl' song which is bound to become a winner. A happy outcome of this encounter is that they give the Outlaws one of the many advertising gifts which are showered upon them. They give the boys a new electric razor, which seems a bizarre gift for eleven-year-olds but is most opportune, as Douglas has recently ruined the one belonging to his elder brother by using it to plane wood to make a model boat. He can now replace it.

A later episode in this book brings William into contact with two sets of Protest Marchers. The local one is nominally organized by the absent-minded but well-meaning Miss Thompson but exists only in her imagination. It is supposedly a branch of the Society for the Preservation of Animal Life, and a Mr Meggison is coming down from headquarters to address what he expects to be a large and lively group. William meets up with a group of very businesslike Protest Marchers who are dying for a cup of tea, and he takes them into Miss Thompson's garden just as Mr Meggison arrives. The marchers are campaigning for freedom in general, but their mascot is Hannah, a pig, which convinces Mr Meggison that they are members of the Society for the Preservation of Animal Life. Everyone is happy, especially the Protest Marchers, who get their tea, sell Hannah, who is becoming a nuisance, to Farmer Smith, and feel that they have really made their mark because 'a boy' – William of course – has asked them all for autographs. In fact, he has made them sign some questionnaires for which a researcher friend needs to obtain signatures.

In *William and the Masked Ranger* we see Douglas, the natural pessimist of the Outlaws, in an unusual role. He has become enamoured of Patsy Willingham, a small girl who lives on the outskirts of the village. '"He's turned into a sort of *slave* . . . He doesn't seem *yuman* any longer,"' says William disgustedly. Douglas abandons the agreeable company of his fellow Outlaws on

"GOSH!" SAID WILLIAM. "YOU'RE THE—"
"ARGONAUTS!" SAID HENRY.

several occasions to be with Patsy, and it is fortunate for the solidarity and survival of the group that the Willinghams do not spend long in the neighbourhood. Even afterwards, when William, Ginger and Henry express their contempt that he has been 'pushin' an ole girl on a swing', etc., the infatuated Douglas still sighs that 'it was a great experience'. His romanticism has hitherto been unmanifest.

In the same book William is feeling aggrieved with the four adult members of his family because they are going to the opening night of the Hadley New Theatre and leaving him at home. His annoyance is twofold; he's interested in the play because it is a thriller, and he'd like to be at the performance because Hubert is bragging that he'll be there in a box. By one of those constant quirks of fate that pursue William from the beginning to the end of his saga, he and the Outlaws, going for a desultory walk on the opening night, run into a young man named Guy Boscastle who turns out to be the author of the play. Depressed at the thought of watching a stage version of his thriller, which has been 'mauled to death' by its adaptor, he decides instead to rush home and start work on the last chapters of his novel, for which William & Co. have inadvertently provided him with inspiration. He offers them tickets for the box which has been reserved for him. Thrilled, they bask in the glory of the stage box, the best seats in the house, which put in the shade those occupied by Hubert's family. Incidentally, in fairness to Mrs Brown, it must be said that William was not left 'home alone'. The Outlaws were invited to spend the evening with him, and given mountains of food which they quickly demolished. At the last moment the grown-up friend of Mrs Brown who was supposed to come and supervise them phones to say that she is prevented. William's family have by then already left for the theatre, and he has no intention of enlightening them and wrecking an evening of freedom for the Outlaws.

In *William – the Superman* (1968) the Outlaws strike a serious note by specu-

"ARE WE ON THE ROAD TO LONDON?"

lating on their being the sole survivors of a nuclear war. 'Come on!' says William. 'Let's think what we'd do if we had to start civilization all over again', which leads to a lively discussion of what is essential to civilization. They propose to establish a primitive settlement, but the other children of the village hear about this and try to muscle in, with Arabella Simpkin, as usual, being obstructive. A TV reporter mistakes the new civilization for a children's play centre and William is prepared to appear on the small screen as the organizer of this. In another episode an aunt of Ginger inspires him and, by extension, the Outlaws to do some service for the community – and encouraged by the aunt's offer of ten shillings if they succeed,

ETHEL WAS GAZING DELIGHTEDLY AT THE BUSTLE DRESS.

William asks what this means: 'Like putting a stop to slavery an' setting up the Health Service an' stoppin' people gettin' executed in public', Ginger suggests. But William points out they've all been done. However, the idea of offering free advice – and earning the ten shillings – appeals strongly, so William sets up a Cittisens Advise Burro. In other stories he starts an Adventure Society, briefly takes up pot-holing and saves an elderly caravan dweller from bureaucracy and being tidied away into an old people's home. The sympathetic old man, his horse and his caravan are reprieved, and the officious social worker, Miss Beedale, is left bemoaning the fact that some of her precious time has been wasted: 'I have every minute of

every day carefully planned, and five minutes lost throws me out for a whole day, if not the week . . .' Unlike William, she has no time to 'stand and stare'.

William – the Lawless was published posthumously in 1970. Richmal Crompton was apparently writing about 'that little savage' until the day before she died in January 1969. Her niece, Richmal Ashbee, found notes and pieces of paper all over the house which she realized were different versions of sections of the story 'William's Foggy Morning' on which her aunt was working. From these jottings Richmal Ashbee was able to finish off this episode, which is included in the final book. William is still tangling with potty causes and campaigns – including the Extra Dimensions and Perfect Harmony Community and a Brighter Thought Movement. These are not quite so hilarious as the Ancient Souls, the gawky Greek dancers, and the intense proponents of elevating ideals that ornamented the William stories of the 1920s and 30s, but the village has moved forward with the times and is now rather more concerned with such matters as the National Health Service, than with the exploration of psychic phenomena. (Most shatteringly of all, the elegant Ethel of earlier decades is now unbecomingly garbed in a mini-skirt.)

Some things, however, do not change. The stalwart citizens and the eccentrics remain to delight us, and the golden glow of William's optimism and sense of adventure still hangs over that nameless, unlocated and universally appealing village:

'Anythin' might turn up,' said William. 'Gosh! There mus' be things turnin' up all over the place. You've only got to find 'em. You don't jus' sit waitin' for 'em . . . I bet people like King Arthur an' Boadicea an' – an' Dick Turpin an' Robin Hood didn't jus' sit around waitin' for things to turn up. They went out an' found 'em . . .'
(*William – the Lawless*)

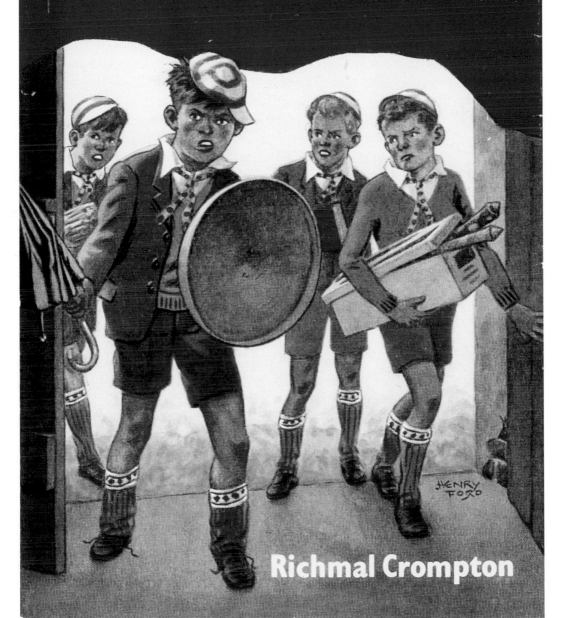

WILLIAM
THE LAWLESS

Richmal Crompton

William Marches Towards the Millennium

After Richmal's death and the posthumous publication of *William – the Lawless* there was, of course, the possibility that with no new stories to come, William and the Outlaws, and all the colourful inhabitants of their village and its environs, might find themselves riding off into the sunset of literary obscurity. Fashions in popular fiction, as in everything else, change and are notoriously fickle. The question of whether or not William might survive for new generations of children and adults seemed also for a period to hang on the uneasy balance between literary assessment and social comment of the kind that is today labelled 'political correctness'.

There is no doubt that William, with his quintessentially English, home-counties, genteel, conservative, middle-class background, and his vociferously expressed xenophobia and sexism, was not exactly the stuff of which acceptable role-models were made for the children of the 1970s and 80s. Many critics and commentators felt that young readers would be more likely to empathize with characters from more ordinary and up-to-date backgrounds, from inner city council estates and large comprehensive schools, who believed in and practised the principles of feminism and social equality. William, perhaps, had had his day . . .

Such critics and commentators reckoned without the extra-ordinary resilience of William, the sparkling satirical style of Richmal Crompton, and the common-sense of past and present, old and new readers who knew a good thing when they saw it and refused to let William and his wonderfully engaging world become extinct. Certainly many of the books went out of print during the 1970s, but collectors in Britain and elsewhere were ardently seeking second-hand copies of William's adventures in the hope of building up the complete set for their shelves. The London Weekend Television series, based on Richmal's stories, in 1977 and 1978 introduced the redoubtable anti-hero to new and very large audiences, and in 1983 Macmillan began to reprint the whole series of thirty-eight William books. By this time many critics welcomed the venture, while others questioned whether the stories which were so expressive of between-the-wars middle-class English life could

A MESSAGE F...

Dear Club Mem...

Mr. Gilliam...

THE OUTLAWS CLUB

TOP SECRET
Do not divulge on
pane. of Deth!

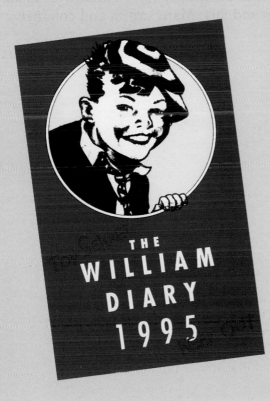

THE
WILLIAM
DIARY
1995

JUST
William's
WORLD
a pictorial map
drawn by Gillian Clements
from a map devised by Kenneth Waller
from Richmal Crompton's 'William' books

possibly appeal to the children of the 1980s. Evidently they *did* strike the right note because sales of these editions are approaching the million mark, they have been translated into several languages, and many juvenile readers have become members of the Outlaws Club, organized by the publishers.

Thomas Henry's exuberant line illustrations (and those of Henry Ford) have been retained in these new editions, but attractive full colour covers by Gerry Haylock are also a lively feature of the series. The last and, for collectors, the most elusive book, *William – the Lawless*, was published in 1993; the reprinted series is thus now complete, and so popular that a new William book was published in 1990, the year that marked the centenary of Richmal's birth. This was called *What's Wrong with Civilizashun* in hardback and, in its paperback reprint, *School is a Waste of Time!* It is a compilation of previously uncollected magazine articles 'by William', expressing his grievances against adult hypocrisy, snobbery, and so on, in his robustly inimitable way. Richmal's centenary year also saw the publication of Gillian Clements's and Kenneth Waller's finely detailed map of William's un-named but atmospheric village (whose location, never revealed by Richmal, has provided enthusiasts with a constant guessing game over the years).

In the stories William – who could never have counted modesty as one of his virtues – boasted that one day the world would ring with his name and that 'stachoos' would be erected in his honour. In fact one was – Graham Ibbeson sculpted it and it was the centre point of 'The World of William' centenary year exhibition at the Bethnal Green Museum of Childhood. For good measure William's likeness was also immortalized in wax at Madame Tussaud's, and in 1993 it adorned thousands of envelopes and postcards when a William postage stamp was issued. In the early 1990s, audio-cassettes of Martin Jarvis's readings of the stories on BBC radio became best-sellers. In 1994 a new William series appeared on our television screens.

There can be no doubt that William Brown – the assertive, insistent, larger-than-life character whom Richmal described as her 'Frankenstein's monster' – will make his resolute way to the Millennium – and far beyond . . .